Other books by the auhor:

Portisville—Novello Award, Fiction
Heart with Joy, Fiction
Hospital Work, poetry chapbook
Midnight Stroll, poetry chapbook

Hopscotch

Steve Cushman

Livingston Press

The University of West Alabama

Typesetting and page layout: Joe Taylor
Proofreading: Joe Taylor, Jacob Glover, Tricia Taylor, Ci Ci Denson, Shelby Parrish
Cover design and layout: Randa Simpson, Callie Murphy, Allie Tittle
Cover photo: Steve Cushman
Author photo: Jan Hensley

Acknowledgements:
I would like to thank the following for help along the way. Of course, Julie and Trevor, because it always starts with you two! Thanks to Debra Coble, Dena Harris, Roger Hart, and Chris Laney who read early drafts and offered valuable feedback. Thanks to Tina Firesheets, Miriam Herin, and Tim Swink for graciously including me in the "four." To Michael Gaspeny, Lee Zacharias, and Mr. O for inviting me into their home on Madison Avenue. And to Joe Taylor at Livingston for taking a chance on this novel, and finally to Liza Fleissig and Ginger Harris-Dontzin who continued to believe in this book long after most people would have given up. Thank you, thank you!

Livingston Press is part of The University of West Alabama,
and thereby has non-profit status.
Donations are tax-deductible:
brothers and sisters, we need 'em.

first edition
6 5 4 3 3 2 1

Hopscotch

for Julie and Trevor

Dr Boles

The first one appeared in the middle of December, on a cool, blue-skied day. It wasn't in a park, on a neighborhood sidewalk, or an elementary school playground as you might expect. It was on the sidewalk leading to the entrance of Alfred Stone Memorial Hospital in Greensboro, North Carolina.

The first person to notice it that morning was an orthopedic surgeon named Dr. Jeffrey Boles. He was talking on his cell phone, asking the OR if his patient was prepped and ready for their total hip replacement, when he looked down and saw it there on the sidewalk.

He stopped. He couldn't quite figure out how, or why, such a thing would be here. But still he found himself smiling as he walked into the hospital to start another busy day.

CEO

The second person to see it was Ralph Davis, the hospital's CEO. He was walking up the sidewalk with Walter Winslow, a member of the hospital's board of trustees. They'd just come from a meeting and the hospital's numbers were down. They needed more patients if they were going to make a profit this year. And for Ralph's job to be secure, the hospital needed to make a profit.

When Davis spotted the drawing on the sidewalk, he smiled for a moment and looked over at Winslow, who wrinkled his nose and shook his head as if he'd encountered something foul-smelling.

"What's that doing here?" Winslow asked, pointing at the sidewalk.

"I don't know," Davis said.

"Well get rid of it."

Davis pulled his cell phone from his pocket and called Jerry Sloan, the manager of the hospital's housekeeping department.

"Sloan, it's Ralph Davis."

"Yes, sir. What can I do for you?"

"There's some graffiti on the sidewalk by the visitor's entrance."

"I'll send someone right away."

Davis hung up without saying goodbye.

Emily

Emily Andrews was eight and small for her age. She had thin blond hair that blended in with the hospital bed sheets. She was in room 302, an IV in each of her arms, and was day-dreaming about cats. Emily had never had a cat but her best friend, Holly Everhart, did. Holly's cats were both white and the only way you could tell them apart was Peanut's tail was shorter than Luna's. Peanut had been hit by a truck when he was a kitten.

Emily remembered playing with the cats back before she got sick. She remembered a lot of things from before she got sick—how she could ride her bike or jump on her trampoline for hours, but she no longer had a trampoline. She'd come home from one of her doctor's appointments and it was gone, as if it had never existed. It was, like most things, something that could hurt her.

The missing trampoline and the trips to the hospital weren't the only differences in her life. Her parents were no longer nice to each other. Emily barely saw them hug or even hold hands anymore. The way her parents treated each other was one of the worst things, Emily thought, about being sick.

She tried to think about silly Peanut again. He loved to chase a piece of yarn and jump up on your belly when you were watching TV and eating popcorn and least expecting it. But she stopped thinking about Peanut because her parents were talking to each other in that voice they used. Short sentences. Whispers. While they weren't pointing fingers at each other, they might as well be.

"I can't," her mother said.

"We don't have a choice," his father said.

"Mom, Dad," Emily called. She knew it would stop them from fighting. They came to her bedside and each took one of her small, bruised hands.

"You okay, Em?" her mother asked.

"Fine," she said. "Let's go for a walk."

Her parents stood on opposite sides of Emily as she walked the halls of the pediatric unit. She liked to see the other kid patients, even if they looked as bad as she did: the yellow masks with the white string around their ears, the bald heads and yellow eyes. The chunky boy with the scar on the right side of his head. This had become her version of childhood and seeing other kids like her made her feel less alone.

As they passed the nurses' station there were two small Christmas trees on the counter, each with acorn-sized gold balls hanging from the branches. And there were stockings and red and green lights hung from the edge of the counter. Emily had been to the hospital a few times before and she had to admit the lights and the stockings made her feel a little better, reminding her Christmas was less than two weeks away.

There was also a miniature Christmas tree on the bedside table in her hospital room and every couple days Emily would find a new treat under the tree. Perhaps a piece of chocolate or some beads for her ever-growing collection of bracelets. This tree was one of the first things she turned to when she woke up each morning.

Emily and her parents passed the game room where there was a full-sized Christmas tree. It had been decorated before she was admitted. It was at least six feet tall, but nowhere near as tall as the huge tree in the hospital lobby.

And while the trees made her smile, they also made her miss her own tree at home. Each year, Emily and her parents would spend the weekend after Thanksgiving choosing and decorating the family tree. It would start on Saturday morning when they drove three hours to a farm in the mountains to find the perfect tree. Her dad would chop it down while her mother paid, and then they would load the tree into the back of his truck. They always stopped at the Denny's, in Boone, for lunch and bought big cups of hot chocolate for the drive home. A drive filled with Christmas music and laughter and her mother singing way out of tune.

They'd make it home by late afternoon and set the Christmas tree up in the corner of the living room. After a big breakfast, the next morning, they would decorate the tree.

Emily had been admitted to the hospital on the day after Thanksgiving, so they hadn't made the trip yet this year. As soon as she got out, her dad said, they'd head up there and buy a tree. But Emily had her doubts she'd ever get out of this hospital, that they would ever make that drive as a family again.

John

John Deaver, the first-shift janitor assigned to the hospital's sidewalks, had spent most of the day with his head down as he cleaned, not looking up, a skill he'd acquired during his time in prison. He was emptying a garbage can by the ED entrance when he got the call on his walkie-talkie. It was his boss, Jerry Sloan.

"John, I need you to go around to the front of the hospital. There's some sort of grafitti on the sidewalk and Mr. Davis wants it removed ASAP."

"Got it." John slid the walkie-talkie back onto his belt and headed to the front of the hospital. He knew he was lucky to have this job. Most people wouldn't hire a convicted felon.

John expected to see some profanity spray-painted on the sidewalk, but he laughed when he saw someone had drawn, with ordinary sidewalk chalk, a hopscotch board in colors of yellow, red, green and blue. By box number 1 was a simple message written in pink: *TRY IT*.

He hadn't seen a hopscotch board in years. The flicker of a memory came to him: Shanna jumping from square to square, her hair in braids. Her feet scuffing the ground. Her sing-song voice.

He called his boss. "Mr. Sloan, the only thing I see is a hopscotch board."

"Hopscotch?" Sloan asked.

"You know, the game with the numbered boxes and you

have to hop from one square to the next without falling over." Was it possible, John wondered, his boss didn't know what hopscotch was?

"Just clean it up," Sloan said.

"Yes, sir. I will."

After collecting the power sprayer from the supply room, John walked back around to the hospital entrance. He wondered who would draw this hopscotch board here. A patient? A visitor? He didn't have a clue.

Before turning the sprayer on, he stepped into the first box. He had hopped as far as box number 5 when he heard a couple doctors talking and walking toward him, so he stepped off the board. Don't screw this job up, John, he told himself. He turned the sprayer on and in less than a minute the board was gone.

Stan

Stan Gordan stared up at the ceiling of room 207, frustrated again. This was no way to live. He'd lost both legs below the knees after a landmine blast in Iraq. He shouldn't have stepped on the landmine. He was ten feet away when he saw his buddy JD heading straight for the blinking red dot beside a rock.

Stan ran at JD with everything he had and pushed him out of the way. All he remembered after that was white-hot heat, a flash, then the swish of a helicopter blade and the medic, a fat Hispanic boy named Jo-Jo, telling him everything was going to be okay.

That was three years ago and the reason he was in this hospital bed smack dab in the middle of North Carolina was because he'd gotten drunk and fallen out of his wheelchair, breaking his right forearm and a couple ribs, along with lacerating his spleen. They had admitted him for a couple days to make sure the bleeding had stopped.

Stan was embarrassed about the fall, about the drinking. He knew he spent too much time feeling sorry for himself, drinking, and playing on-line poker. He'd won a Purple Heart for his bravery and sacrifice in that far-away country, but every time he looked down at his legs, which ended in stumps below the knees, he felt as if his life was over, that the best parts were behind him now.

Stan's brother, Jay, told him he needed to get himself together. He needed to get a job, something to do everyday, then he would start to feel better. Jay even offered him a job at the insurance company he managed, but Stan didn't think he could stomach pushing paper for the rest of his life.

Instead, he spent a couple hours a day staring out the window of the house he shared with Jay, watching the rest of the world walk on by. He watched the young mothers push their baby-filled strollers down the street, the retirees walk their small dogs, and the men and women joggers. The mailman, a tall thin guy with a mustache, dropped the mail off between 2 and 2:30 every day. He watched these people take their legs for granted and it made him angry.

He sat up in the hospital bed, transferred to his wheelchair. He rolled the three feet to the window and looked out at the naked trees and spotted the same red-tailed hawk he'd seen for the last two days, flying around the perimeter of the hospital as if on lookout. Stan turned to the sidewalk where a man in a white lab coat, a doctor perhaps, but not one Stan recognized, was hopping from leg to leg on what looked like a hopscotch board.

Stan turned away to the TV, looking for a sitcom with canned laughter, some show that would take his mind off yet another thing he would never be able to do again.

Mary

Mary Jones stood beside the hospital bed in room 403, where her husband, Walter, was sleeping. He had pneumonia. She hated to see him like this. He was old now, 84, but he'd always been so active, a high school basketball coach. But now he looked as if he could slip away from her at any minute.

Mary had enjoyed the drive to the hospital because she could pretend for a little while, at least, that she was not on her way to stand beside her dying husband, but heading to her bridge club, to the grocery store, or even the mall to buy her grandchildren Christmas presents.

Mary wished she could shake Walter awake and make him go for a walk with her. But every time he moved he went into an ugly coughing fit. Maybe tomorrow, she thought, maybe.

She remembered the long walks they would take in the early years of their courtship. He always held her hand and made her feel protected, leaning into her shoulder, the two of them running to a lake in the middle of the summer, fully clothed, and jumping in. The shock of the cool water. The laughter.

Mary wiped the tears from her eyes. Where did all that go? Where did he go?

While she knew it wasn't his fault, she was still angry he was here, that they were here, in a hospital and that she had become a stranger to him. She hated how he treated other people, even strangers, nicer than he treated her. She was not ready for this. It was not fair. This whole damn thing was not fair.

"Walter," she said. "Walter." When he didn't respond, she squeezed his forearm to rouse him but all he did was cough once and moan slightly.

"Wake up," she said, leaning forward so their faces were only inches apart. "It's always about you, isn't it? Basketball and your precious teams and now this. For once in your life, can't it be about somebody other than you? Don't you dare leave me like this."

Mary began to shake. She told herself to calm down. And for the hundredth time, she told herself it wasn't his fault. She walked to the window and lifted it a couple inches to get some fresh air. Outside, on the sidewalk below her, Mary spotted a teenage girl with short black hair, hopping. It seemed an odd thing to see at a hospital, so Mary blinked twice and looked harder, only then realizing the girl was jumping on what looked like a hopscotch board. A teenage boy walked up and took the girl's hand and together they disappeared into the hospital.

The memory that came to Mary was so raw and full of joy she had to sit down in the chair beside the bed. It was Christmas break, 1951, over sixty years ago. They were college seniors. She was at the Woman's College of Greensboro while he was at the University of North Carolina in Chapel Hill. He'd gone there on a basketball scholarship and he'd done well his first two years, but a knee injury in the 2nd half of a game against NC State had ended his playing days. She remembered him telling her this in one of the long rambling letters he sent her once a week. He said now that he couldn't play he would like to coach basketball, teach others about this thing that had always mattered so much to him. He'd said he wanted to give other kids the joy and pleasure of a basketball court and teammates he'd been lucky enough to have.

It was two days before Christmas, cold but not freezing, and they both wore jackets and corduroys, gloves and hats, as they walked around the neighborhood. She had still not bought him anything for Christmas and was trying to decide if she ought to get him a new sweater or some cologne, maybe a journal for writing notes or letters to her.

The houses they passed were decorated with Christmas lights, and while it was mid-day, they could see lit trees through windows. They could hear Christmas music. Mary felt warm and comfortable with Walter beside her. The neighborhood was only two miles from the Woman's College where both of their fathers were professors.

They turned a corner, and there by the Hughes' big white house, someone had drawn a hopscotch board with pink sidewalk chalk.

"Let's play," Walter said.

"I don't know," she said. Her mother had told them to be back in ten minutes for lunch.

He smiled at her, then walked over and picked up one of the blue stones in the brown grass. "I'll go first," he said, tossing the stone, hopping forward, making it to three until he fell over into the grass. Because he was grabbing his knee, she'd thought he might actually be hurt, so she ran to his side, tried to help him up, but he pulled her down on top of him.

They laughed and he kissed her there on the grass. He pulled something from his pocket, a small black box. "I was going to wait until Christmas, but this seems like too good a chance to let pass by." He held the box out to her, opened it, and there was a ring. An engagement ring shining and silver and the diamond just the size she would want.

"Will you, Mary Ann Bousquest, be my wife forever and ever?"

And then she was crying and laughing and hurrying back to her house to share the good news with her mother and father and little sister.

Stan

Stan turned away from the window when he heard his hospital room door open. He'd been watching one of the hospital's janitors hopping down there on the hopscotch board. Earlier it was a doctor and now a janitor.

"Hey, Bro," Jay, Stan's brother, said. He was in one of his fancy grey suits, a perfectly healthy 28-year-old with two strong legs.

After Stan's recovery and rehab at the military hospital in Salisbury, Jay drove him to his house in Greensboro, said Stan could live with him there. He'd built a wheelchair ramp and re-arranged his house to accomodate the wheelchair, but instead of being grateful all Stan felt was anger. It wasn't fair that he would have to live like this: other people making decisions for him, his life in a damn chair.

"How you feeling?" Jay asked.

"Just dandy."

"You gotta wear the cast for a month?"

"Maybe longer," Stan said.

"I guess we'll miss the Charlotte 5k," Jay said.

Since Stan had been home, Jay had been after him to enter one of those races where all the contestants were in wheelchairs. There was one in Charlotte in March, but Stan knew he couldn't practice now with a broken forearm.

While he'd never told his brother, Stan had tried a few times to race around the block as fast as he could, to try and gauge what it might be like to race in his wheelchair, but each time he was amazed at how much it had taken out of him. His hands blistered and bled and his heart pounded, so he drank a beer and popped a pill for the relief it brought, for the way it stopped the buzzing in his head and chest.

But this led to more beer and he would pass out and Jay would come home from work and get angry with him for drinking and Stan wouldn't tell him what he'd done that day, what he'd tried to accomplish. It was after his fifth training session that Stan had gotten drunk and fallen out of his chair and hurt himself.

"Maybe next year," Jay said

"Forget it, man. I'm not going to go out there and look like a freak. I'm not going to race." Stan had had enough.

"Come on, Stan."

"Are you blind? Can't you see I don't have legs? Can't you see that?"

"Of course, I can," Jay said, rubbing his forehead as if he had a headache.

"Please just leave me alone."

When Jay didn't move, Stan pushed the chair as fast as he could into the wall. He backed up and did it again. He wanted to scream. He wanted to be left alone. He could feel the blood in his arms, in his chest, his face felt like it was on fire.

Stan's face was wet with sweat, tears on his cheeks.

He'd done a good job of making himself look mad, mean, and angry. It worked and it kept people away from him, kept them from offering to help him. Everyone, that is, except for his brother.

"I'm not going anywhere," Jay said. "Stop feeling sorry for yourself. There are people worse off than you."

"You don't know what it's like to be trapped in this chair everyday."

"I wish it was me, brother, but it's not," Jay said. "You still have a life, a different one, but you still have a life."

A nurse came in and asked if everything was alright. After she left, they both looked out the window. It was easier than trying to talk. They watched a couple kids, a boy and girl, jumping on the hopscotch board. The tension seemed to lift as Stan took a couple deep breaths.

Jay spoke first. "Do you remember when we used to play hopscotch?"

Stan didn't say anything. He was tired of saying things. He was tired of pushing himself around. He was tired of looking down where there should be long, strong legs. He hated shoes. He hated what he could never get back. And he hated how a girl he'd planned to marry, Clarissa Koehler, told him a week after his return home from the VA that she couldn't marry him now, that she just couldn't imagine taking care of him for the rest of her life.

He remembered beating his brother in hopscotch, even though Jay was two years older. Jay was the smart kid while Stan was the athlete, playing baseball and football from kindergarten all the way through high school. And because he could beat Jay, Stan would draw a hopscotch board on the driveway and they would play before their father got home from work, parking on top of the board.

Stan wondered why his brother had continued to play

with him. Did he think he would actually beat him one day? Or did he do it because he was the older brother, the one his parents talked about with the good grades, and he wanted to give Stan this? Stan didn't know, but he remembered feeling a confidence whenever they played and he won.

"Yeah, I'd kick your butt," Stan said.

"I let you," Jay said.

"Whatever."

"Well, I bet I could beat you now," Jay said.

And because it was such an awful and perfect thing to say, they both laughed harder than they had in a long time. "We'll see about that," Stan said. "Let's go."

"Where?"

"To get some fresh air."

Stan led the way, down the hall to the elevator, and out the door to the sidewalk where that hopscotch board was drawn in yellow, red, green and blue chalk.

"You toss the stone, and I'll jump for you," Jay said.

Stan felt something lift in his chest as if he were taking his first real deep breath since landing in this wheelchair. His brother had taken him in, had even remodeled his house so it would be easier for Stan to live there. He didn't have to do any of it, but he had.

Stan took a stone from the Styrofoam cup on top of the garbage can. He tossed the stone and it landed on the one.

If Jay was not athletic when they were children, he was even less so now. He tried to hop and lost his balance, almost fell over. This got them both laughing. Stan rolled his wheelchair up beside him and cheered his brother on, throwing the stone marker and calling the numbers out.

Emily

After circling the pediatric unit twice, Emily and her parents went back to her room. She was usually tired after her short walks and went straight to bed for a quick nap, but today she walked over to the window and looked down. On the sidewalk, there were two men. One was in a wheelchair, and the other in a suit. The man in the wheelchair threw a stone onto what looked like a hopscotch board, then the other man hopped from square to square.

Of course, she'd played hopscotch in PE. She'd even played it with Holly Everhart, but Holly usually won.

Her parents walked up beside her and looked down to see what she was watching. She could feel them look at each other, over her head, and she knew what they were thinking: something else she can't do.

Mary

Mary wondered more than once over the years if Walter had drawn that hopscotch board on the sidewalk, if he'd planned the whole thing. She'd asked him about it a couple times and could never get a straight answer. If she had to guess, she'd say he had. He was the sort of man who planned things like that, surprises for other people's benefits.

That hopscotch board in their old neighborhood was not the last one she would see. A kindergarten teacher for over two decades, she had taught hundreds of children how to play the game. And with each new year, as she explained the rules to the children, she couldn't help but think of

Walter and that Christmas he'd asked her to marry him.

"When's breakfast?" Walter asked now, adjusting himself in the hopsital bed and coughing. He hadn't said anything in over an hour and it was almost time for lunch. He'd eaten breakfast, four pancakes smothered with maple syrup. The man could still eat and eat, but quite often he didn't remember who she was.

Their three children had been telling Mary for the past year that it was time to move him into an assisted living facility. They didn't think she could take care of him anymore. He would wake in the middle of the night, calling for her, and she would say I'm right here, and he would ask who the hell she was and what had she done with his lovely Mary. He'd fall asleep and not remember any of it in the morning.

The doctors she'd consulted said it was a gradual slipping away that would only get worse. The medications they tried had not helped, and they all agreed it was time to seriously consider some sort of assisted living facility. Many of these places, they said, had apartments where spouses could live and be near their loved ones. She had not been ready for that, but she knew now that if he did leave the hospital she would have to consider one of those places.

"Breakfast?" he asked again.

"Walter, it's me, Mary. Lunch will be here soon."

He stared at her face as if he were about to recognize her, but then he shook his head and closed his eyes, his lips in a frown. She studied the lines in his face. Every morning for almost six decades, he had sat across from her at breakfast and ate the eggs and toast she made for him. They would talk about whatever was going on in the world—had talked their way through three wars—and he would go off to work, to teach children social studies, sometimes using the things he discussed with his wife as a springboard for class discussion.

And how he loved to coach basketball. Some nights during basketball season he would not get home until after nine. She would bring him dinner wrapped in foil, drop it off in his office for that twenty to thirty minutes he had between the end of the school day and when practice or games would begin.

But she had loved their long summers together. A few glorious weeks each year where she could take him away from the long hours of school and basketball and they would travel to Cape Cod, New York, Vegas, London, Ireland, even Hawaii. Once the children grew up and moved away Mary and Walter would spend their summers visiting them in Iowa or Illinois or Florida. A pair of accountants and a stay-at-home mom. She never quite understood how two of her children became accountants but figured it was only one of the gazillion things she didn't understand.

Like Walter's brain. Where did it go? How was it possible all those memories could slip away to nothing? It wasn't fair, but nothing was fair, Mary Jones, she told herself again, so stop your whining. You've had so many good years. Yes, you have.

When the nurse came in with the lunch tray, Walter sat up and offered her, this stranger, his first real smile of the day. Mary took a deep breath, reminded herself that it wasn't really her Walter anymore. He had, she was afraid, already gone far away.

Emily

"I want to do that," Emily said. She pointed down at the sidewalk and the men on the hopscotch board.

She knew her parents were choosing their words, trying to find the right way to say she couldn't. She was too fragile. She was "immuno-compromised" now because of the chemo. That's why she had to wear the yellow mask all the time. And she couldn't have any visitors who had a cold or were sick in any way because she could easily catch their colds or whatever germs they had. At least, that's how it was explained to her.

"I'm not sure it's a good idea," her mother said.

"Come on, Bev," her dad said. "We won't be out there long. The fresh air might do her good."

"The fresh air might not do her good," her mother said. Emily knew her mother was really saying the fresh air might kill her. But this was her life and Emily knew she probably would not get to grow up and be a teenage girl who falls in love with a boy, and eventually gets married and has children and a home of her own she could decorate any way she wanted. And while, of course, this scared and saddened her in ways she couldn't understand, it was the life she had, and she needed to do something while she was still here.

Emily turned back to the window. Her mother was the cautious one, afraid that everything she did could end in disaster, everywhere she turned landmines lay in wait, ready to go off, and her father was the opposite: he wanted her to do things before it was too late, he'd had to practically beg her mother to take that trip to Disney before they started treatment again. She knew they both loved her in their own ways and were both trying to do what they thought was right.

Still, she couldn't take this anymore, so Emily turned and ran for the door.

"Emily," her mother said. "Emily!"

But she was already gone. She ran so fast the IV lines ripped out of her arms. The medicine sprayed the air. She was running now and she could hear her parents behind her, but they would have to drag her back. She couldn't stay in that room anymore. She ran by the elevator. She ran by the stairs, tripped and fell on the hard floor.

She couldn't see any of the nurses or other kids now, but she could hear her parents' cries, along with someone coughing down the hall. Emily could feel them behind her. She grabbed the closet door handle, ran inside and locked the door.

They were banging on the door. Emily looked around. There were cleaning supplies and boxes of gloves, piles of new linen. She reached up and pulled one of the sheets off the shelf. She wrapped herself up in the sheet because she was cold. Her arms were wet where the blood had flowed out. She pulled her mask off and threw it on the ground. Her legs ached now, pinpricks along both knees. She'd grown used to the fact that some part of her body always hurt.

Outside, they banged on the door. She would not let them in. She would stay here for as long as she could.

Rosa

As Rosa Hernandez turned onto Elm Street, her *La Vida Loca* ringtone chimed. She shook her head and pulled her green BMW into the parking lot of an apartment complex. As a local TV newscaster, she had done more than her share of reports on people killed in car accidents while talking on their cell phones, so she never talked on the phone while driving. She assumed the call was from her husband, Ray. They'd just had lunch, but it hadn't ended well. They'd had the same *have a baby now or wait* conversation they'd had a dozen times before. He was ready for children, but she was not.

"Hello," she answered.

It was a man, but it was not her husband. "Come to the hospital," he said. "There's something you need to see and report on."

"Who is this?" she asked.

But he had already hung up. Rosa wondered if he worked with Ray, who was a pediatrician.

She turned around and drove back to the hospital where she had just dropped Ray off. During lunch, she had tried to make it clear to him the reason she wasn't ready for children was because she wanted to establish herself as a newscaster before becoming a parent. While she wanted children, she knew that now, in her late twenties, was the time to build her career. She had every intention of being a great mother when the time came.

Pulling into the hospital parking garage, Rosa sat in her car for a moment, considering whether or not she should call Ray and tell him she was here. He had been fine with not having a child while he was in med school and even into his residency, but now that he'd been in his practice for three years and was working relatively normal hours, he was ready to be a parent. That, Rosa had said, was all she was waiting for: the right time.

In her rear-view mirror, Rosa brushed her hair and

applied fresh lipstick. Being on TV for an hour everyday meant people often recognized her in public. Some of them treated her like an old friend and would stop her and want to talk, while others only stared. Either way, she had to look good. It came with the job.

Rosa walked past two men, whom she assumed were brothers, on the sidewalk by the hospital entrance. They were both in their late twenties and one of them was in a suit, the other in a wheelchair. It looked like they were playing some version of hopscotch where the man in the wheelchair would throw the stone and the other one would hop.

She thought it was strange that she'd been to this hospital a hundred times and had never noticed a hopscotch board drawn on the sidewalk.

The first thing Rosa spotted in the atrium was the huge Christmas tree. It was exactly 33 feet high, something she knew because she'd reported on the lighting of the tree a couple weeks earlier. One of the volunteers was playing *Silver Bells* on the piano in the corner while a half dozen employees ate their lunches at small, square tables.

Rosa looked around, not sure what she was expecting to see. Had she thought that man on the phone would be standing here, waiting to tell her what she was supposed to report on? She didn't think so. Again, she considered calling Ray or going to see him up on the Pediatric unit, or maybe even walking around the hospital, trying to find out what this thing was she needed to see, but decided to head on to work. She had a lot to do before the five o' clock telecast.

Back outside, she looked over at the hopscotch board, but the two men were gone. She wondered for a moment if they had been there at all. If she had imagined them. But the hopscotch board was there, clear as day. Had it really, she wondered, been there all along and she'd missed it?

While she didn't hop, she did step in each square, feeling better than earlier, after her lunch with Ray. She headed back to the station, to work.

Emily

Emily was cleaned up and back in her hospital bed with a pair of new IV's in her arms, a new gown. She had stayed in the supply closet for almost five minutes before a man from hospital security came and unlocked the door. By then, she was too tired to fight.

She was asleep in her hospital bed when the door opened. She assumed it was her parents, but instead it was Dr. Soodapong, her pediatrician, who had told Emily to call her Dr. S. She was a petite, older lady whose black and white hair always looked a mess. She reminded Emily of a small, female, Asian mad scientist. And she always pulled a lollipop from her lab coat pocket and gave it to Emily. Always, every time, even when the girl was so sick she couldn't possibly lick a lollipop.

"How are you today?" Dr. S asked.

"Okay."

The doctor tilted her head sideways. "I don't like that answer, Suzy Q."

Emily assumed she called all her girl patients Suzy Q because she had walked by a patient's room where Dr. S was talking to another little girl, and she'd also called her Suzy Q.

"So why did you run away?"

"Look out there," Emily said, pointing toward the window.

Dr. S walked over to the window. "I see a sidewalk. The tops of trees. Lots of leaves on the ground."

Emily laughed. "No, silly. Look at them, down there."

Dr. S took off her glasses and looked harder. She rubbed her eyes, opened them wide and looked again. "I don't know what you mean, Suzy Q."

"There are two men playing hopscotch."

Dr. S shook her head. "You going crazy on me, Suzy Q? Do we need to scan your head? You are seeing things that are not there."

Emily climbed out of bed and walked over to Dr. S and the window. She looked down at the sidewalk. Dr. S was right. The two men were gone. Of course, she thought, it had been at least an hour since she'd seen them. "There were two men out there playing hopscotch. One was in a wheelchair."

Dr. S sat on the bed and tapped the sheet beside her leg as if to say come here, sit down. When Emily did, Dr. S hugged her. "You're a special girl, my Suzy Q. You need to go outside. You need to smell the air. Being in a hospital room for too long messes with our heads. Is that why you ran?"

Emily started crying and told her she hated being in the hospital. She hated not being able to see her friends or play with her neighbor's cats, about how she was tired of having needles in her arms, about the strange smell inside the yellow mask. And she told her how she wanted to go outside and try the hopscotch board, but her parents wouldn't let her.

"Oh, Suzy Q. They love you. They are worried." Dr. S hugged her again and took out her prescription pad and started to write. She handed the prescription to Emily and kissed her on the forehead. "If what you want is to hop, hop, hop, then let's go hop, hop, hop." She waved for Emily to follow her.

Emily looked down at the prescription in her hand. It said: *Have fun, go outside and play 2 x a day.*

Dr. S held out her hand. Emily slid on her pink parka, took the doctor's hand, and they walked out into the hall. Her parents were sitting in the waiting room, an empty seat between them, not talking. Both parents looked up, surprised to see Emily and the doctor standing there.

"Let's go," Dr. S said. "Suzy Q here wants to hopscotch."

Her mother started to say something, but Dr. S said, "Doctor's orders." And Emily handed the prescription to her mother, who shook her head and smiled despite herself. Together, they walked to the elevators in a straight line: Emily, her doctor, and her two loving, scared, and confused parents.

Emily had not been outside in over a week. The air felt crisp and cool—mid fifties—but not too bad for December. While Dr. S held her hand, Emily could hear her parents' whispers behind her, and she was waiting for them to say *Stop, we can't be outside, we must get her back inside.* But they didn't say anything.

Emily heard birdsong. She could hear cars on the road nearby, and she could hear a man, around the corner, talking on his cell phone. She could hear the not-so-distant siren of an ambulance. She could smell some sort of dark incense.

The hopscotch board was practically worn away, and Emily assumed it was from the wheelchair rolling over the lines. "It's almost gone," Emily said.

Dr. S squeezed her hand. "Oh, Suzy Q. We can't give

up that easy."

Dr. S found a piece of pink sidewalk chalk on top of the garbage can and re-traced the lines of the board. "Now, Suzy Q, you hop. I've got to go and see other children." She handed Emily a red lollipop.

As the doctor started to walk away, Emily's mom asked, "Should she really be out here?"

"Why not?" Dr. S asked.

"Her immune system."

The doctor hugged her and said, "Oh, Mrs. Andrews, you've got to let her live a little."

Dr. S turned back to Emily. "Have fun, Suzy Q," she said as she walked back in the hospital's entrance, rubbing her own arms for warmth.

As Emily's father stood beside her, her mother walked over and sat on the bench. Emily tried to look away because she didn't want them to see her crying. She knew they would think something was wrong, but there was nothing wrong. Her family was together and she was about to play a game she hadn't played in a long time.

"So remind me," her father said. "How do you play this game?"

"You toss the stone or rock or whatever you want to use as a marker into box number 1, then you have to jump all the way to the end box, number 10, where you can rest for ten seconds. Where there is one box by itself you have to hop on one leg, but where there are two boxes side by side—like the four and five and the eight and nine here— you can land on both legs. After your rest period, you have to turn around and hop all the way back, picking up your marker along the way. Then you throw it into box number 2 and do the whole thing again until you are able to throw it into the last box and hop all the way there and back."

"What happens if you don't toss it into the right box?"

"You lose your turn," she said. "And have to wait until the next person goes."

"So whoever goes all the way to the end and back wins?" he asked.

"You got it."

"Sounds easy enough," he said and turned to Emily's mom. "Do you want to play, Bev?"

She shook her head and folded her arms across her chest as if to warm herself.

"Come on," he asked again.

"No," Emily's mother said.

"Your loss," her father said.

Emily went first, tossing her stone into the first box. She laughed and started to hop. She almost fell and when her father reached to catch her she laughed and said, "It's okay. I'm okay."

Metalhead Mike

Metalhead Mike drops the Wii remote in the Pediatric playroom. He's had enough for today. Mario and Sonic are giving him a headache. All the bright colors give him a headache. Heck, there's not much that doesn't give him a headache anymore. And the plates in his head, the thirty-two stitches, make his head itch like you wouldn't believe. Some days it takes all the strength he has not to just itch and itch and itch.

The window behind him is bright with light. That's another thing he can't get used to. The lights. But he sees the bare trees outside and walks toward the window.

Surely he must have climbed trees, but he can't remember ever doing that. There is so much he can't remember.

Outside, on the sidewalk below, he sees a girl and her father. The girl has blond hair and is a few years younger than he is. She looks familiar. Her father stands beside her as she hops along the sidewalk.

Metalhead Mike's Auntie Michelle and Uncle Bobby keep telling him his parents are away on a trip, but he's not dumb. They would have come back by now. They wouldn't leave their son in the hospital for 27 days. At least that's what it says on the chalkboard in his room—*Length of Stay: 27 days*—but to him it could be 1 day or 100 or 27 days. It makes no difference.

He knows what happened to his parents. Sort of. He remembers the white light. The heat. The smoke. The darkness. Waking up in a hospital bed with an itchy head. But he wants to know what happened right before. He knows the secret is there, hidden away in some deep crevice of his mashed up brain. He just has to find a way to get to it.

But why in the world is that girl and her father hopping around on a sidewalk? It doesn't make any sense, not that much makes sense to him anymore.

Back in his room, Metalhead climbs under the sheets of his hospital bed. He likes to play a game he's made up called the Memory Game. It works like this—in the late afternoons when he is tired from his physical therapy or the bright lights in the hall he climbs into bed and turns off all the lights and put his head under the heavy, warm covers. He closes his eyes and tries to remember whatever he can about his parents. Sometimes memories come and other times nothing, only a darkness that eventually leads to him drifting off for a quick nap.

The memories, when they come, usually play out in his head like a scene from a movie and feature a boy he assumes is himself and a pair of adults with blurry, undefined faces that he assumes are his parents.

Today, he's thinking about that girl hopping along the sidewalk as he starts to nod off. For some reason that makes no sense to him, he sees an empty porch swing, swaying slightly, a window cracked and the curtain swishing in and out, like a breath.

It has to be Christmastime because he sees the decorations on the porch, the red and silver balls twirled around the porch's wide columns. And he can see the un-lit Christmas tree through the window. He's at the steps, selling cookies or something, holding a plastic bag. He's walking up the tall steps in a heavy blue jacket. At the top, he notices a big, brown dog, napping on a yellow pillow beneath the open window.

For a moment, Metalhead freezes. He doesn't think he's afraid of dogs, but he stops when the dog opens his eyes, a little at first and then a great deal wider. He stares at Metalhead and Metalhead doesn't move, waiting to see what the dog will do. Eventually, the dog only closes his eyes and returns to his nap, his big face resting on a front paw.

Metalhead ties the plastic bag around the old, brass door handle. A few strands of silver and gold tassel litter the porch floor. Beneath his jacket, Metalhead wears a blue button-up shirt covered with round and square and oval patches. When he turns, back on the sidewalk, there's another boy dressed just like him. Metalhead runs down the steps to the sidewalk and the other boy and a man in jeans and a red jacket, a yellow and blue Cub Scouts hat. He thinks he was in Cub Scout Pack 160. He thinks they met at that church a mile or so from his house.

And Metalhead is sleeping, dreaming, walking along a sidewalk that could have been in his neighborhood, or another state, or something he only remembers from a movie. Whether any of it was true, or part of his actual past, he doesn't know, but that's how the Memory Game works. He's not sure he'll ever know the truth, but for these flashes he's grateful, a sign he's lived a life before this one, and hopeful they'll help him remember it all, under the dark covers of a hospital bed that has become his home away from home.

Dr. Boles

Dr. Boles walked out of the hospital, chilled by the evening air. It had been a busy day. He'd performed three surgeries along with applying a cast to a little boy's left ankle in the ER. But he still had to go home and change and make himself presentable. His wife was having one of her dinner parties. Secretly, he'd hoped some emergency might keep him at the hospital, but none had come, so it was time to go.

For Dr. Boles, trying to make conversation with his wife's friends was much harder than performing surgery. In the OR, and at his office, he felt comfortable. In just about every other social situation, he felt uncomfortable. But he knew why.

His work had defined him and had given him and his family a good life, but it had also isolated him. All those hours, late nights and weekends, he had spent in surgical scrubs, a mask across his face, bent over a broken bone or a mangled knee. Bones didn't talk. They were either straight or not. And his job, plain and simple, was to make them straight again.

But his work had cost him. He'd missed much of his son's, Myles' life. The boy was five, starting kindergarten, and then he was ten, and twelve, and Dr. Boles didn't know what to say to him.

He remembered walking by Myles' room one day when the boy was fifteen. The sound of a guitar met him in the hall. It was an acoustic guitar and Dr. Boles eased the door open. Myles was sitting on his bed, playing with confidence, his fingers dancing across the strings, his head nodding in a steady, sure rhythm. Dr. Boles had stood there for no more than a minute, amazed at his son's ability, disappointed in himself for not knowing his own child could do something like this.

Dr. Boles shook his head as he walked up the sidewalk. He spotted that hopscotch board again. The lines were a little off-center, the boxes not exactly perfect squares, but still.

He remembered playing the game as a boy, growing up in Pinellas Park, Florida. He tried to remember if he'd ever seen his son playing hopscotch, but he couldn't. He hadn't been there the first time Myles had ridden a bike or when he hit his first home run in little league. He hadn't been there for much of the boy's youth. And now Myles was in his second year of medical school, out in California.

Dr. Boles took a deep breath and headed to his brand new Range Rover and took the long way home, hoping his beeper would go off, allowing him to turn around and head back to the safety and comfort of the hospital.

John

At the end of his shift, John walked by the sidewalk where the hopscotch board had been. His boss, Sloan, had called him an hour earlier and told him the hopscotch board was on the sidewalk again, that he needed to go back and erase it.

Like before, John wondered where it had come from and who would draw it here, at a hospital. Probably some kid visiting a sick parent. But to have someone draw it twice today didn't make sense unless someone had drawn it on their way into the hopital and again on their way out. Either way, the board was gone and the sidewalk was clean. He'd erased it as if had never been there at all.

He sat down on the bench beside the board and took a few deep breaths. If he could only erase certain parts of his life, he thought.

Shanna, his daughter, had been seven when it happened, almost ten years ago now. He was a year from finishing his accounting degree and had gone to an end of semester party at his favorite professor's house with his wife, Tara. They'd had a great time. There were so many people at the party, and he was so close to the life he'd always wanted. While he only drank three beers in two hours they were enough to dull his senses. He was driving, not speeding, just driving, both hands on the wheel. They were two blocks from his house when the possum ran out in front of them.

John swerved the car, sending his Ford Escort into an oncoming pickup truck. While the driver of the truck was not injured, Tara was killed instantly. John broke his right femur and was a patient at this very hospital for a week. When he was released from the hospital, he went to jail for DUI and involuntary vehicular manslaughter. Tara's family wanted every possible charge brought against him. The courts gave custody of Shanna to her grandparents, Tara's parents, when he went away to prison.

Sitting on the bench, John remembered what his prison psychologist had told him: when it feels like the world is about to explode, just take some deep breaths. And, of course, John's guilt over what happened to Tara was strong and sure and held him tight. Almost every night when he was in his little apartment, lifting weights and watching TV, he would see her in the car beside him, her eyes still open, her head turned a little too far to the side. Her eyes seemed to say *How could you,* and John could only think I'm sorry, I'm sorry.

No matter how guilty he felt, Tara was still gone. And he'd missed seeing his daughter grow up. Yes, he tried to contact her. He sent letters once a week. He called so many times that Tara's parents had his calls blocked. He hadn't given up hope. He'd continued to send letters. He'd continued to try and call.

Two weeks before his release, he received the notice that he was not allowed within a mile of her. If he did approach her, it would be a violation of probation. He'd go back to jail.

What little he knew about Shanna, came from his sister-in-law, Angelina. She told him Shanna worked part-time at a Hardees in Winston-Salem and she wanted to be a nurse. John had grown a beard and wore a baseball hat and went to see her on Tuesday evenings where she worked.

He'd ordered the same thing, a burger and fries with a small Diet Coke, and he'd sit there and eat and watch her, both relieved and disappointed that she hadn't recognized him. And he imagined what her life was like, what their whole family would have been like if he hadn't swerved to miss that possum, if he hadn't had one drink too many. He imagined a house with a garage. Shanna would have her own room and they'd buy her a little car, something small but safe.

The *what if's* were what got you. What kept you awake at night when a sane person would somehow learn to let it go. To somehow get on with their life. But John couldn't see how he could ever let this go. He knew there was no excuse for what he'd done—drinking and driving—but he was not a bad man, only someone who had made a mistake, a mistake that had cost him dearly, that would cost him each and every day for the rest of his life.

John reached over and picked up a piece of pink sidewalk chalk and drew another hopscotch board on the sidewalk. He knew he'd probably have to wash it away again tomorrow, but it would be there for a little while. Maybe a kid would smile. Maybe they'd even laugh because of something he'd done.

CEO

The next day, on his way to another meeting, Davis spotted the hopscotch board again. He stopped right in the middle of it, one foot on the four, the other on the five. He thought of the conversation with Winslow the day before and tried to scuff the chalk out with his shiny black loafers, but it would take more than a pair of $300 shoes to get rid of this.

He imagined his two girls having fun, hopping on this. What would it really hurt to leave it here? But he shook his head and that thought away. First a hopscotch board, then what? A basketball court? Merry-go-round? A jungle gym? What if one of the patients fell and was injured? No, it had to go. This was a hospital, not a playground.

He called Sloan again.

"Environmental Services," Sloan answered.

"It's Davis. Didn't I tell you to clean this sidewalk graffiti?"

"Yes, we did."

"It's back. I want it gone now."

"We'll be right there," Sloan said.

John

John was not surprised when he got the call from Sloan, saying to clean the hopscotch board again. John wanted to tell his boss that he'd re-drawn it the night before and that if he had to erase it and draw it again later he'd be glad to, but he said no such thing. When John arrived at the sidewalk, there was a little girl, a patient in a hospital gown, hopping on the board. The girl's mother and father stood off to the side and watched her. John could see the nervousness in the mother's eyes, the joy in the father's. He could hear the little girl's laughter. Job or no job, he would not deny this little girl. He'd come back in a little while and clean the sidewalk.

Rosa

After her morning workout, Rosa checked her voice mail. There was a message from the same man who called the day before, saying there was something happening at the hospital she needed to see. Part of her wondered if she should report this to her boss, but the caller hadn't sounded mean or threatening.

She called Ray and asked him if he knew of anything unusual going on.

"Nope," he said. "Just a bunch of sick kids up here."

She respected her husband because he helped so many kids, and he loved doing it. That was one of the reasons this whole start a family thing was getting to her. He rarely asked much of her. Soon, she'd told him more than once, soon she'd be ready.

"Did you need anything, Rosy?"

"No, that's it."

"I gotta run. I've got a boy down the hall trying to get himself on a ventilator."

"Love you, Ray," she said.

After hanging up, Rosa decided to swing by the hospital again. This time, as she walked from the garage to the hospital she noticed a girl, obviously a patient with a hospital gown under her pink jacket and the yellow mask, hopping on the hopscotch board. The girl looked up at her and smiled, lifting the corners of her eyes over her mask.

"I've seen you on TV," the girl said.

"Yes," Rosa said. "That's my job. I'm Rosa. What's your name?"

"Emily. Emily Andrews."

They shook hands and Rosa said it was nice to meet her. The girl's father waved to Rosa while her mother turned away.

"Did you draw this?" Rosa asked, motioning toward the board.

Emily shook her head. "I saw it from my window." She turned and pointed up toward a window.

"We came down here yesterday and again earlier today," her father said. "Emily likes it. It gets her out of that room upstairs."

"Have fun," Rosa said. "And Merry Christmas."

"You too," Emily said, then went back to her game.

After another uneventful walk around the hospital, Rosa considered going upstairs to visit Ray, but figured he was probably busy. When she walked out the front door, the little girl was gone. Rosa sat down at the picnic table over by the parking garage and checked her cell for messages. She noticed a doctor in a white lab coat walk by the board and stop. After looking around to make sure no one was watching, but missing Rosa, he jumped his way across the boxes, before heading to his car. The fact he'd tried to hide what he was doing made Rosa smile.

Rosa was about to leave when the automatic entrance door opened and those two brothers she'd seen the day before appeared again. The one in the wheelchair wheeled over to the board and grabbed a stone. He tossed it as his brother did the hopping for him. Is this my story, Rosa wondered. While it was certainly touching, she wasn't sure it was an actual news story. Either way, it was getting cold and time for her to go.

Mary

Mary served Walter his breakfast of pancakes, and the whole time he ate and chewed and stared into her eyes without recognition. She turned to the window again.

This time there was a little girl hopping on the sidewalk. Her parents were standing off to the side, watching her. Mary watched for about five minutes, noticed how the mother wanted to run over and help, but the girl had her IV pole for balance.

Even in the brief time Mary watched her jump, she could tell the girl was getting tired. She was not jumping as high or as far, and she seemed to require a few more seconds of breathing to recover between each hop. It wasn't fair. She'd seen so many kids play this game with little to no effort.

When the girl was done playing, each parent held her by the elbow and they disappeared around the corner, out of sight.

"Let's go," Mary said.

"Huh?" Walter looked up as if realizing for the first time she was in the room.

"We're going for a little ride."

"Does my doctor know about this?"

"It was his idea," she said, feeling a tinge of guilt for lying to him. But she had to get out of here. She held his arm and helped him ease into the wheelchair from the bed. He looked at the chair and snarled, shook his head. Mary wrapped him in his jacket and put a sheet over his legs.

When they passed the nurses' station, Walter asked if anyone had seen his wife.

"She's right there, pushing you, Mr. Jones."

Walter looked back at Mary and shook his head, as if to

say *No, that's not her.*

"If we're not back in an hour, send out a search party," Mary said, trying to lighten the mood.

Walter's nurse only stared at Mary, not getting the joke. But Mary needed to get him outside, see if he responded in any way to seeing the board.

More than once, during their walks through the years, they had come across a hopscotch board drawn by some kid on the sidewalk. And each time, Walter would take her hand and they would try to hop together. It had been over a year since they had seen one of these boards.

He didn't say anything as she pushed the chair, didn't perk up as they went outside and hit the cool air. For a moment, she stopped there at the exit door, wondering if she was doing the right thing, if she ought to just turn around and get him back to the safety of his hospital room. No, she wouldn't turn around yet. This trip was important. She had to do it. He needed it too. She was sure of that.

She imagined him standing up, shaking off his weak legs and walking hand in hand with her. How she missed their walks. In the ten years since his retirement, they had rekindled their habit of walking together. Once in the morning and again in the evening they would go for twenty minute walks. Sometimes they wouldn't say a word, other times they would comment on the houses they passed or what was going on with their kids, their grandchildren, the world around them.

Even these walks had stopped a couple months ago when he'd started sleeping more, his mind seeming to close in on itself. He'd look at her and ask if she was his long dead sister, sometimes his assistant coach, sometimes his daughter, but rarely was she his wife, Mary Jones, anymore. And now, here he was, in the hospital with pneumonia. A nice, long walk, hand in hand, sounded like a slice of paradise to Mary.

When they found the hopscotch board, the little girl was gone. On the ground, beside the board, were two small plastic cups: one held pieces of pink and blue sidewalk chalk and the other a half-dozen quarter-sized stones.

Seeing the board this close, Mary felt a quick jolt through her chest. It took her a moment to catch her breath, so she led Walter to the bench and sat down beside him. He stared at the board, his head tilted to the side a bit as if he were trying to figure out what it might be.

"Do you remember?" she asked.

"Huh?" was all he said, and then he said it again.

Mary sighed and shook her head. She had walked him out here for what? He was not going to recognize her. He sat there, staring forward, not the least bit aware of, or interested in, what she was referring to. She picked up one of the stones, figuring why not. They were already out here. It was a nice day. She tossed the stone and hopped with both feet, felt the tinge of pain in her right hip.

She glanced over at Walter before every move, but his face was as soft and blank as a slice of Wonder bread. Where had he gone? Where had his mind taken him? As long as he was not in pain, she told herself, and there was no reason to suspect he was, except when he started with one of his coughing fits.

She would try one more time, then they would go upstairs. She'd tuck him into bed, and she would go out by herself for an hour or two. Maybe she would sneak away to a movie, not that she had any idea what movies were playing. First things first. She threw the stone and hopped again. Then she heard it, "Mary?"

His voice was soft, questioning. She walked over and kneeled in front of him. He reached out and touched her wet cheeks. "My sweet Mary Ann," he said. "Where have you been?"

"I've been here," she said. "Oh, Walter. I've been here all along."

He squinted and shook his head as if trying to figure out what was going on. He reached out and they hugged there on the sidewalk. She sat on the bench beside his wheelchair, holding his hand. She told him why he was in the hospital, and about their life. He asked about their children, even got their names right for the first time in what seemed like forever. He asked her if she'd taken care of all the Christmas shopping for the grandkids and she'd said she had, which was not entirely true.

When he said he was tired, she pushed the wheelchair, taking the long way around the hospital, trying to hold on to this moment, extend it out beyond where they'd been before. She told him about all the basketball teams he'd coached, about the two players who'd gone on to play in the NBA, about the boys who had gone on to be coaches and police officers and teachers too. She told him he was a wonderful basketball player himself, that he could jump higher than any man she had ever met.

Back in his room, she helped him into bed, pulled the covers up to his chest.

"Get some rest," she said. "I've got to go make some phone calls."

He said her name three times. "Are you coming back?"

She smiled. "Yes," she said. "I'll be back. I promise."

She was at the door, when he said her name again, "I've missed you, Mary."

"Oh Walter, I've missed you too."

He closed his eyes and she thought, sleep well, my prince, sleep well.

Metalhead Mike

Metalhead is under the covers again, after an hour of physical therapy, playing the Memory Game. This time he's in his kitchen, looking out the back window and there's a man standing outside in front of a pair of sawhorses. He is bent over, sawing a plank of wood. He has on jeans and a green shirt and an Atlanta Braves baseball cap. Metalhead thinks this is his father, but he can't say for sure.

He turns to the table and sees a picture cut from a magazine of a small wooden fort. Metalhead doesn't have a fort, has never had one, but he's asked his father to build him one. That's what his father must be doing. Metalhead watches him for a few minutes, the way he grips the wood, his shirt already spotted with sweat on this Saturday morning. At least he assumes it's a Saturday because why else would his father be out there instead of at work in one of his suits?

In a minute, Metalhead will go out and help him, but first he is hungry. He wants some cereal, so he grabs a box of Cheerios and milk and eats while he watches his father, watches the muscles in his arms as he works the saw over the wood. Metalhead can see the shape of the pack of cigarettes in the right shoulder sleeve of the T-shirt. He can see the birds—small, red and black birds—on the feeders there beyond his father's shoulders and the other bird—the kind with the orange chest—in the birdbath.

He can see all of this around his father, as if he, too, were a natural thing in their backyard. And for some reason, at that moment, Metalhead's father looks back at the house, at the kitchen window and straight at Metalhead. He has a cigarette in his mouth and he raises a hand to wave and Metalhead waves back.

His father mouths some silent words, and Metalhead lifts his cereal bowl in an answer, as if to say I'll be there as soon as I finish this. His father shakes his head and turns back to work. Metalhead finishes the bowl of cereal, sits at the kitchen table and begins to play his videogame. A few minutes later, the back door opens and his father is running inside, his face white, his hand and T-shirt covered in blood and he is moving toward the sink, saying come on, we've got to go to the hospital and Metalhead is saying, *What, why, what happened?*

Mary

Mary closed her cell phone and slid it into her purse. She took another sip of the hospital cafeteria coffee. Yes, Walter had recognized her, had come back for a few minutes, but she knew he would only recognize her on occasion. The rest of the time he would stare at her, not knowing who she was and why she kept trying to talk to him. It was time for him to go into a nursing home, or assisted living facility, or whatever they wanted to call it. She would still see him everyday, but there would be professionals at those places that could take care of him. She had gone ahead and made an appointment with the social worker to start the process.

When the elevator door opened on Walter's floor, she

knew something was wrong. Walter's nurse ran past her, pushing a big orange cart. She turned to Mary, opened her mouth as if she were going to say something but didn't. Mary watched the nurse push open the door to Walter's room and drag the cart inside.

Without meaning to, Mary walked slower. She wanted to turn around and go back downstairs into the cafeteria, back to those moments before the elevator door opened, back when things finally seemed to be going in the right direction.

Dr. Thompson, Walter's doctor, walked out of the room. He looked up at her and shook his head just enough to tell her Walter was gone. He held his arms out and Mary accepted his hug.

"I'm sorry," he said. "His heart."

"Can I see him?"

"Give us a few minutes."

He led her to a consultation room with framed posters of flowers on the walls and boxes of tissues on the table.

Mary closed her eyes and thought of that day Walter had asked her to marry him. It was a magical day, so many years ago. She wondered if everyone had days like that. How you can turn a corner and fall into something better than you'd ever expected.

Emily

It started with a little sniffle, a cold, then a fever. Emily missed a few days of school and her mother kept saying it was no big deal, just a little bug. But after a few days of fevers over 100, they went to the pediatrician, a tall, hairy man named Dr. Felsner. As her mother described her symptoms, the doctor made eye contact with Emily, and the look she saw in his face was not good, but he did eventually turn away, offer her a sort of half smile. He lifted Emily's arms and he pressed his hands into her arms pits and Emily flinched from the pain.

Emily remembered him sighing, as if it was painful for him too. "We'll get some labs," he said.

"But it's just a cold, an upper respiratory thing, right?" her mother asked.

"That's what we're hoping for," he said, turning away and writing something on a prescription pad. "Let's start on some antibiotics and see what the labs look like. I'll call you tomorrow when we get the results."

Again, Emily and the doctor made eye contact. His eyes were soft and blue, but there was something about them that struck Emily as a little scared. Like before, he followed the moment of eye contact with a quick, well-practiced smile.

It was the first time Emily had ever given blood. It scared her. The phlebotomist's white, paper gown. The purple tourniquet squeezing her arm. Her mother's smile. And the needle, the quick pain she knew was coming, but still wasn't ready for.

"All done," the lady said, untying the tourniquet with one hand while shaking the vial of Emily's blood in the other. Emily smiled when the lady gave her a Dora the Explorer Band-aid, even though she had stopped watching the show a couple years earlier.

She spent the rest of that afternoon sleeping on the living room couch, watching a little TV whenever she woke. The medicine was pink, like a strawberry milkshake, but didn't taste good at all. She hoped she could go to school the next day, but when she woke in the morning her mother said they had to go back to the doctor's office. This time her father went too, which Emily thought was weird because her father usually didn't go to doctor or dentist appointments with her.

Dr. Felsner smiled again at Emily. "Why don't we have Susan here take you down to the treasure chest and let you pick something." The treasure chest was a big, old box with toys for the patients.

Emily looked back at her mother once before leaving the room with the nurse. What she remembered was how big her mother's eyes were. The way she folded her arm across her chest as if to protect herself from whatever news the doctor was about to deliver.

Emily took her time, looking through the stickers, the small plastic cars and stuffed animals, dogs and cats and lions. A few minutes later, the door opened and her parents were walking toward her with a stack of papers and they each took one of her hands and walked out, quickly, without saying anything to anyone, not even the nice white-haired lady at the desk who usually scheduled Emily's next appointments.

In the car, Emily said, "Are we going home?"

Her parents looked at each other. "Not yet," her mother said. "We have to go to see another doctor."

"Why?" she asked.

"Because Dr. Felsner," her mother started and stopped. "Said he wants another doctor, a specialist, to look at you."

Five minutes later, they pulled into a building with a sign that said, Central Carolina Cancer Center. And in this way, Emily began to understand what was happening. Not that she knew what cancer was, only that both of her grandmothers had died of cancer. This, whatever it was she had, was not a cold or the flu. It was something much worse.

John

It took him three bus transfers and over an hour to travel the 20 miles from Greensboro to the bus stop closest to the Hardees in Winston-Salem where Shanna worked. He had vowed while in prison he would never drive a car again. His driving had killed his wife and caused so much pain for those left behind. He'd gotten the apartment two miles from the hospital so he could walk to work. And while he didn't think he'd work at the hospital for the rest of his life, he did think he would always work close to his home, wherever that might be.

The bus pulled to a stop. It was not a particularly nice part of town but once you spend time in prison any place is better than being in there. Every time he walked toward the fast food restaurant, he felt a flash of mixed emotions. Part of him wanted to run in there and say, 'Hi Shanna it's me, Dad.' But the other part knew it was best if she didn't recognize him. He had been out of her life for ten years and he couldn't be sure how she'd react. It could land him back in jail because of the restraining order and push a wedge deeper between them. And what if she hated him? She certainly had every reason to. Accident or not, it was his fault her mother was dead.

He took a deep breath, opened the door, felt the restaurant's stale heat hit him. There she was, leaning toward a customer as the lady ordered. Shanna looked like her mother, thin and awkwardly tall, definitely the tallest kid working there. She had a quick smile and easy laugh. Today, she was wearing a red Santa hat with her name in gold cursive along the white border. Her straight black hair curled out from beneath the hat.

John walked to the counter, which was decorated with red and green tassle, a silver ball, hanging from each cash register. His heart pounding. His eyes trying to take in every detail of her face—the tiny mole above her right eye, the long soft eyelashes, her perfect brown skin and emerald earrings—because he wouldn't see her for another week.

"Can I help you?" she asked.

He pulled the brim of his hat down a little, though she had never shown the slightest flick of recognition in the twenty or so times he had walked up to her register. With the hat and beard and oversized, blue work jacket, he knew he looked like a different person than the father she had known.

"Cheeseburger, fries, and small Diet Coke," he said. He hoped his voice was not shaky.

She rang him up, told him the amount. He handed her the money, held it a second too long, hoping to brush her hands, but she was quick and deftly took the ten dollar bill and gave him his change without touching him at all. He remembered holding her hand and walking to school.

He remembered one day when they had found a baby bird on the sidewalk. It was small and brown and half-feathered and it was obvious the bird couldn't fly. John had picked it up and set it back in the nest as the mama bird squawked. For weeks afterward, she insisted they walk by that same tree to make sure the bird was okay. When they saw a sparrow flying near the tree, she would ask if one of them was the bird they'd helped, and he would say it was certainly possible.

And he remembered her first day of kindergarten. Tara was so nervous. Shanna walked away from them, tall and proud, with her teacher, Mrs. Nedmons. But Tara cried in the school cafeteria after Shanna disappeared around the corner. He hugged her until they were one of the last sets of parents left there.

John took his tray and went to sit in a booth. He sat in the same booth every week because it offered him an unobstructed view of the counter and Shanna. He didn't stare because he didn't want to scare her or draw any attenion to himself. He never stayed more than fifteen minutes, just the normal length of time he thought a customer might need to casually eat a cheeseburger and french fries.

As he ate, he watched the way she talked to customers and how she joked with the other teenager employees. He imagined what her life was like. Did she have boyfriends? Did she have a hobby? Did she do good in school? Was she happy? What sorts of things did a seventeen-year-old girl want for Christmas these days? His sister-in-law only told him so much, but he was grateful for what little she did give him.

When his time was almost up, he took a deep breath and let it out. It would be another week—seven days, one hundred sixty eight hours—before he'd get to see her again. At least now he could be in the same room as her, even if they had to be strangers. He wiped his eyes and stood to leave. After emptying his tray into the garbage can, he walked back to the counter and asked for a refill, then smiled at her once more and left.

Stan

It was time for Stan Gordon to go home. As they waited for the nurse to get the discharge paperwork together, Jay showed Stan a flyer he'd printed off the internet for a wheelchair race four months away in Asheville. That should be enough time for him to get out of the cast and build up strength in his broken arm. He knew his brother had done a lot for him, more than he had ever expected. If Jay wanted him to enter one of those wheelchair races at least he could try. It would be a lot of work, but Stan thought a trip to the mountains sounded like a good idea. He hadn't been to Asheville since he was a teenager, and this gave him something to look forward to.

Jay was on his cell phone, explaining to someone that he would be at work around noon, as soon as he got his brother home and settled in. Stan wheeled over to the window again. Outside, on the hopscotch board there was a young blond girl. Her parents stood beside her. When the girl tilted to one side, her parents reached out to steady her. Stan thought of Jay down there hopping for him, being the legs he no longer had.

Stan turned around as his nurse walked toward him with a stack of papers. She walked up beside him and looked out the window. "Hopscotch?" she asked.

Stan nodded. "Where did it come from, the hopscotch board?"

She shrugged her shoulders. "Don't know," she said. "You take care of yourself."

Jay pushed Stan out the door and onto the elevator. They headed over to see the hopscotch board before leaving. Since first discovering the board three days ago, they'd spent at least an hour out here each day. And for

Stan those hours had been some of the best of his life since he'd stepped on that landmine. He'd actually laughed and had fun with his brother.

The little girl was still out there. Her parents were standing off to the side. Her father was clapping while the mother held a box of tissues in her hands. And the little girl held onto her IV pole as she hopped. The pole, and her parents close by, seemed to offer her all the balance and support she needed.

The two brothers watched from a distance. They didn't want to disturb this family. But when the girl spotted Stan and Jay, they started to clap for her. The parents looked up at them. The girl bowed and smiled under the mask, her eyes raised and brighter for a moment. She waved and Stan waved back and the brothers turned around and started back up the sidewalk, heading home.

Sara

Sara didn't want to go to the hopsital. It was where people went to die. Her grandmother and her Auntie Donna had both died in this hospital.

And now her daddy was supposed to have some sort of procedure on his heart. According to her mother, it wasn't an operation, but Sara didn't understand exactly what it was. All she knew was her daddy hadn't been home the last two nights. They'd decorated the Christmas tree, he'd gone in to work the evening shift, but he hadn't come home.

As they pulled into the hospital parking deck, Sara could feel her own heart thumping hard and steady in her chest. She imagined the blood her heart was pumping through her whole body.

Sara's mother held her hand as they walked across the parking deck toward the hospital entrance. Her mom was acting brave now, but Sara had seen her a couple hours earlier, sitting at the kitchen table, drinking her coffee and crying. Sara hadn't said anything to her then, had simply walked back to her bedroom and read her *Junie B. Jones* book until her mother called for her.

After a shower, her mother put on her happy face, full of smiles. Sara was scared though. She'd seen her mother, heard her whispering on the phone. Her daddy wasn't an old man. He wasn't even fifty. He exercised and ate healthy so none of this made sense to her.

Christmas was usually her favorite time of the year. Of course, she loved the gifts her parents bought her, but what she liked most was the cookies her mother made for Santa, the red and green sweaters all her friends wore to school and how she got to visit her grandparents and see all her cousins. Even that snooty-patooty Jillian from Charlotte. But what she wanted this year more than anything was for her daddy to be home.

Sara thought of her Auntie Donna. She loved Auntie Donna. She had been a nurse and had long, straight black hair. Auntie Donna got some sort of cancer. One night, Sara and her parents had come to visit her in this hospital. Auntie Donna told her that she should never be afraid, that she had loved being a nurse and she hoped Sara too found something she loved to do.

That was three years ago, back when Sara was only five, so she didn't really understand what Auntie Donna meant. The next day Sara's father sat her down and told her that Auntie Donna was gone. She had died in the night. She would not be coming home.

That was Sara's last memory of coming to the hospital. People come here, and then they die.

Sara heard someone laughing. Her mother was holding her hand as they walked toward the entrance. It took Sara a moment to figure out who was laughing and clapping. On the sidewalk, beside the hospital entrance, a girl about her age was playing hopscotch while her father clapped with each hop she took.

It was obvious the girl was a patient because you could see the hospital gown under her pink jacket and a yellow mask covered most of her face.

Sara pulled on her mother's arm and they stopped.

"What?" her mother asked.

She pointed to the hopscotch board, to that little girl. "Can I?" Sara asked.

Her mother looked at her watch and nodded. "Just for a minute, Sara. It's cold out here."

Sara walked over to the hopscotch board and the other girl, who said, "Hi, I'm Emily."

"I'm Sara. Can I play with you?"

"Sure," Emily said.

They stood there for a second, both wanting the same thing, just someone to play with to help them forget they were standing in this place neither one wanted to be.

Sara's mother sat down beside Emily's parents. And for a few minutes, the two girls played a child's game with crooked boxes and stones and all the simple, hopeful things that make up a hopscotch board.

The girls laughed and cheered each other on, but they didn't talk about anything in particular. They held hands between throws and when it was time to go, Sara said her daddy was upstairs and they were going to visit him.

Emily wished her good luck.

At the entrance to the hospital, Sara turned back to wave, but Emily had already started another game. She was jumping again, full of life, holding on to what she had left.

Rosa

As soon as she wrapped up her morning show, Rosa drove over to the hospital again, curious to see if other people were using the hopscotch board. So far she had seen that little girl, those brothers, and a doctor. She had two free hours before her mid-morning meeting with Ed, her producer, for the noon broadcast. She usually spent that time running errands or going to the gym. But she was intrigued by the hopscotch board and wanted to figure out if this board was the story her mystery caller was talking about.

She sat at the picnic table again, beside the parking lot, about twenty yards from the hopscotch board. When she first sat down, no one was at the board, but within five minutes that little girl, Emily, walked outside with her parents and started to play. This time she didn't have her IV pole and Rosa didn't know if this was a good sign or not.

While her mother sat on the bench, with her arms folded tight across her chest, Emily's father played the game with her.

Rosa watched the people who passed the Andrews family on their way into the hospital. Whether they were an employee or visitor, almost everyone smiled at the girl. And Rosa realized at that moment what the board offered, hope: hope for life, hope for recovery, and hope for happiness.

A girl walked up to Emily and while Rosa could not hear what was said she must have asked if she could play because Emily nodded enthusiastcially. They only played for a few minutes, but it was enough time for them each to go to the end of the board and back twice. The girl hugged Emily and went with her mother inside the hospital.

After Emily and her parents left, other visitors and staff would stop at the board, hop a few boxes and go inside to work. Rosa watched a man in a grey suit and brown fedora hat, a visitor she assumed, stop at the board, squat down and trace the hopscotch board's lines with the sidewalk chalk before walking around the corner.

Her cell phone rang and Rosa pulled it from her purse.

"Hello," she said.

"Thanks for coming." It was the same voice as before.

"Is the hopscotch board what I'm supposed to see?" she asked.

"Very good," he said. "Spread the word on this."

"Who are you?" she asked.

"That's not important. You've seen how it affects people. That's what's important." And then he was gone.

Rosa looked around. She wasn't afraid. The voice never sounded threatening. For all she knew it could have been any of the fifty people that had passed her in the last hour. It could have been that man who bent over and traced the outline of the board again. She didn't know. But she knew she did have the power, in her job as a reporter, to get the word out.

Every day, she reported the news someone else prepared for her, and most of it was bad news (car wrecks and robberies and murders), but this was her chance to show people something good, introduce them to something positive right here in their own community.

She called Janice Adams, her contact in the hospital's PR department. They'd worked together on different stories and hospital events, like the 5K run for prostate cancer survivors, over the last couple years. When Janice said she didn't know anything about the hopscotch board, Rosa told her to come check it out, and Janice promised she would after her morning meetings.

"I'll call you after I go see it," Janice said.

"Sounds good."

Rosa didn't have much time before she had to be back to work, so she called Ray, asked him if he could steal away a few minutes. He said he'd meet her in the lobby.

She told him about the phone calls and that she'd been watching people for the last hour. "It's interesting," she said as she led him out the door toward the board. "People walk by it and about half of them stop. It's like they're mesmerized. They can't ignore it. Maybe it means something different for each person. Maybe it brings back their childhood, or memories of their own children, but whatever it is, it seems to take them away from their worries, even if just for a few moments."

As if on cue, an older woman walked out of the hospital. She was carrying a green baseball hat in one hand, tissue in the other. She stopped at the board and while she didn't throw any stones or hop, she tilted her head to the side and closed her eyes and smiled as if she were remembering something.

Rosa and Ray didn't say anything until she was gone, walking off into the parking garage. "See," she said. "People can't walk by it without stopping. Do you have any idea who would have drawn it there?" she asked.

"It could have been someone who works here—maybe a physical therapist, a chaplain—or someone just visiting. Maybe a little kid was tired of sitting in a room with one of his or her parents and decided to draw it out here. I'll ask around upstairs. Maybe some of my kids who are able to go outside can come out here and play."

She liked that he called his patients *my kids*. He had done it as long as she had known him, almost eight years now.

Rosa told him about the little blond girl, Emily Andrews. Ray said she wasn't one of his patients, but he knew about her and it didn't look good. When Rosa asked what he meant, Ray hugged her and said they were doing everything they could but her type of Lymphoma was pretty aggressive.

She kissed Ray on the cheek and told him she'd see him later. He started for the door and turned toward the board and hopped on one leg across the board. At the end, he put his arms out and bowed to her. Rosa smiled and waved.

She knew she was a lucky woman to have him and that he would indeed make a great father. Before walking to her car, Rosa stopped at the board and re-traced the lines on the sidewalk, adding a little heart inside box number 6.

Sara

Sara was relieved. Her daddy seemed okay. He was in a good mood and had joked about needing a shave. They said the procedure had gone well, and he should be released in a day or two. He'd definitely be home for

Christmas. The doctors had put something called a stent in his heart. When the doctor showed her a pictue of a stent, Sara thought it looked like a tiny Slinky.

As they reached the lobby, Sara thought of Emily, that girl she had played with earlier. She hoped she was out there, so they could play another game. But she wasn't. There were no other kids around.

"Want to play?" her mother asked.

Sara turned toward her mother. She was smiling now. She had been so nervous earlier when they'd arrived at the hospital. Sara grabbed two stones from the styrofoam cup and gave one to her mother. They played for a few minutes. It was good to see her mother laugh. It felt good to hop here on the sidewalk and know her daddy would be coming home. Soon, they would all be together again as a family.

Rosa

After finishing her noon broadcast, Rosa called Janice to see if she had gone over and seen the hopscotch board.

"I agree with you. It is cool," Janice said. "I hadn't noticed it, but I don't usually go in or out of the hospital that way."

"I was thinking of doing a report on it," Rosa said. "It would be good for the hospital."

"It sounds like a great idea," Janice said. "Let's do it. I don't think Davis, the CEO, will have any problems with it. I'll call him."

Rosa hung up the phone and went straight to Ed's office. Ed was a short man with glasses and a crew cut.

The only decoration in his office was a dartboard on the wall. The three darts were always in the bullseye, and Rosa wondered if he was really that good at the game or if he had stuck the darts in there and never moved them.

"What's up, Rosa?" he asked.

"I've got an idea for a story," she said.

Ed leaned back in his chair. While he had not agreed to do every story she'd suggested, she always felt like he listened to her. She told him about the hopscotch board, about the people she'd seen there and the mysterious phone calls. She told him about the little girl, the man in the grey suit, and the brothers. She told him this thing, a child's game, was making a difference in people's lives.

He listened and nodded and said okay. "Let me know when you're ready to do it, and we'll schedule it. People love this sort of feel good stuff."

"Thank you," she said and thought, *That was way too easy.*

Margie, RN

The nurse had seen the hopscotch board when she'd walked into work that morning. There had been a couple teenage girls jumping on it. When she came outside to take a break, she noticed the board again. There were no kids on it, but there was a bird. A mockingbird. The bird hopped from square to square in no particular order. Of course, he wasn't actually playing the game. Or was he? She didn't know but it was enough to put a smile on her face. A bird playing hopscotch. Who'd ever heard of such a thing?

Emily

The nurse smiled at Emily. The nurse's name was Juliet. She had short blond hair and chubby cheeks and blue eyes. While Emily had been taken care of by a lot of nurses, she thought Juliet was nice because she told Emily about her six month old baby, Trevor, and about the horses her husband trained. She said that once Emily got out of the hospital she could come over and ride one of the horses. Plus, Juliet never said this is not going to hurt when she was about to do something that would hurt. Emily had learned that just about everything they do to you in the hospital hurts.

Emily felt the tourniquet tighten on her right arm as Juliet rubbed her skin with the cold alcohol pad. Emily turned away as Juliet popped the plastic cap on the needle. Since Emily had to have a new IV every few days she'd almost gotten used to this. Almost.

"A pinch and burn, my girl," Juliet said.

With her free hand, Emily squeezed her mother's hand. She squeezed back. Emily could feel Juliet's fingers on her forearm and knew the jab was coming. She closed her eyes and saw the hopscotch board's lazy squares. The numbers written in orange. The sidewalk chalk. Then there was a quick, sharp pinch. Emily was laughing and her mom and dad were hopping and laughing. Her friend Holly and her two cats, Peanut and Luna, were there playing on the hopscotch board too.

"Great job," Juliet said. "All done."

Emily looked up. Her mother was smiling at her, but Emily closed her eyes and searched for that game of hopscotch she'd just begun in her head. She could feel the cool air. She could hear a car honk somewhere and there on that sidewalk, hopping and laughing, was a little girl and that little girl was her.

Metalhead Mike

Metalhead closes his eyes, tries to ease the headache away. Auntie Michelle has gone back to work, and he's climbed under the covers. All he can see are the red dots on the backs of his eyes. He blinks twice. He is standing next to a white square on the ground. It's a base, third base. He knows this because the dugout is to his right. Along the dugout fence, there are black and silver and purple bats. The glove on his hand is too big, but his father said he'd grow into it. There's a boy up to bat, but Metalhead is too busy kicking the dirt to notice.

He's done 12 figure-eights in the orange clay with his cleats. His record is 20, so he tells himself to hurry. He hears the clink of ball meeting bat and looks up as the ball rolls toward him, a small white circle traveling through air and grass and a second or two later it rolls to a stop there at his feet. He can hear everyone screaming, calling his name, so he bends down and grabs the ball in his bare hand. Instead of throwing to first, he steps on the base beside him.

There are more screams, people clapping. He sees his mother, or at least a woman he assumes is his mother, on the bleacher outside the fence. She's wearing a big, brown gardening hat, so he can't really see her face, but he knows it's her, the long black hair on her shoulders, her hands outstretched as if reaching for him.

The coach, on the pitching mound, tells Metalhead to

throw him the ball, so he can pitch to the next batter, but instead Metalhead walks over and drops the ball in his glove.

Back in his position beside third base, Metalhead has finished three more figure-eights before his teammates start to run off the field, so he follows them to the dugout where the coach says, "You're up next, Mike."

Metalhead finds a batting helmet and the purple bat with his name written on it in silver Sharpie, and he takes a few practice swings. He's not so good at fielding, but he knows how to hit. There's an old tire in his backyard that he's hit many, many times, practicing. His father tied it to the tree, showed him how to swing, how to find the sweet spot.

He's standing at the half triangle-half square of home plate, waiting for the pitch. His grip is strong on the bat. He can hear a woman calling out to him, telling him to take his time and hit that ball. The coach looks at him and nods, asking if he's ready, and when Metalhead nods yes, the coach throws the ball at the plate, at him, at the catcher's mitt.

Metalhead swings and the ball flutters on by. "Keep your eye on it, Mike," the coach says.

He thinks the coach might be his dad. Tall, with a dark beard, blue shorts and white tube socks. While he can't see them from here, Metalhead knows his father's arms are covered with dark hair. Hair, Metalhead remembered pulling at when he was younger, back when the two of them would spend Saturday mornings on the couch, watching cartoons.

The next ball is coming and Metalhead is staring hard. He can see the red thread, the white shape coming his way and when it gets there he swings, swings so hard he thinks the ball will disappear up into the sky and never return. He swings so hard that his helmet flies off his head but he doesn't hit the ball. The catcher has it and is throwing it back to his father.

Metalhead adjusts the helmet again, not sure how he missed that one. He's mad his helmet fell off, but his coach/dad says, "This one, you'll get this one."

Metalhead grips the bat. It's one of those perfect spring days with a stop at the ice cream shop on the way home. Pistachio and vanilla mixed in a waffle cone. The ball has left his father's hand. It's coming and this time Metalhead knows he's going to hit it. He knows. He swings the bat, knowing this time he will make that ball fly.

Emily

With her new IV in place, Emily and her parents headed outside to the hopscotch board. Occasionally, as Emily hopped, she could feel the pinch of the needle in her arm, but she tried to focus on something else. When she looked over at her parents, she saw them as she always did—her father's goofy smile and her mother's tight, nervous lips.

It was odd that it was the lips she always focused on, but there they were—different yet the same and she was hopping, lifting one foot, then the other. For a few minutes she did not want to let anyone else hop. This was hers; this hopscotch board on the sidewalk below her hospital room. Her lungs were filling with the crisp December air, burning her chest in a good way. And she could feel the sweat through her T-shirt, gown and jacket.

Suddenly, she felt herself slide forward, could feel her

front leg extending a bit too far and she was tumbling into the IV pole and falling forward. She hit the ground hard, unable to extend her arms because of the IV's. She came down on an elbow, her right hip, the side of her head. At first she didn't feel anything, but then there was a sharp pain in her elbow and on the right side of her face. She could hear her mother screaming, "Emily! Clay, go get help!"

But before he could even get inside the hospital, a nurse who'd just wheeled another patient outside to go home, ran over with a wheelchair. As they loaded Emily into the wheelchair, her mother kept saying, "I knew it. I knew it."

They started for the inside of the hospital. Emily wasn't so much in pain as she was shocked. She could feel something wet on the side of her head and knew it was blood. Her mother kept saying, "Not this now. Not now."

They helped her back into her bed, and Juliet, her nurse, came in and helped clean her up. Emily was a little dizzy. She thought she was going to be sick and then she was sick and her mother was wiping her forehead. Dr. S walked in the room. "Oh, Suzy Q, what are we going to do with you?"

Emily heard the doctor's voice change as she spoke to her parents. It was less playful. There was no mention of Suzy Q. "We'll do some X-rays," the doctor said.

"I knew we shouldn't have let her. She's never going on that thing again," Emily's mother said.

"It was just a little accident. She tripped. Let's not make a federal case over this," her dad said.

"We don't need this now," her mother said.

"Bev, that's enough. Stop it. There is probably nothing wrong, just a few bumps and bruises."

When Emily slid into the CT scanner, she wasn't scared. She had been scared a year ago, when she had her first scan, but now this had become part of her life. She even sort of liked how you slid into the donut, how you were protected from the world in there, a cocoon, and then the machine started. She could hear the low rumble, the sound of a motor. And Emily began to cry. She was not scared of being injured, but she was afraid she might not ever get to go out on that hopscotch board again.

She knew she was not hurt, not seriously. She'd hit her head before, felt dizzy for a few minutes, but then it went away. She felt the same now. But maybe if they had the CT and it showed everything was okay, her mother would let her play again, but she knew how stubborn her mother could be.

Emily thought it was her own fault for falling. All she had to do was hop like she'd done a hundred times before. It was that IV pole that had tripped her up.

When they slid Emily out of the CT machine, she wiped her eyes, tried not to let them see her crying, but it was no use. The X-ray girl smiled at Emily and handed her some tissue, said she was going to bring her to a different room so they could do the X-rays on her elbow.

John

After leaving work and going home, lifting weights, taking a shower and eating dinner, John walked the two miles back to the hospital. Above him the stars were bright. It was a cool night, and he could hear an occasional snippet of music coming from the houses he passed. He thought of that little girl he'd seen out on the hopscotch board the last few days and wondered what was actually wrong with her.

He hoped she would be okay. He didn't know anything about medicine, but he was doing what he could to help her. He was going back to draw that hopscotch board so that when she came out in the morning it would be there for her.

He walked past the parking garage and up the sidewalk. When he reached the strip of sidewalk where he had erased the hopscotch board once again before leaving work, he stopped and smiled. Someone had already re-drawn it. John laughed. It felt good to laugh.

On his walk back home, he stopped beneath an overpass. He still had one of the pieces of sidewalk chalk in his pocket, so he pulled it out and drew a board there on the sidewalk while above him cars roared by.

John smiled and slid the chalk back in his pocket. It felt good to draw the board here, even though he knew this was not a sidewalk many children would walk on. Still, it felt good to create the possibility of someone using this board.

Emily

An hour after Emily returned to her room, Dr. S came by and said the CT scan looked fine. "No damage, just rang her bell a bit. Elbow X-rays were normal too."

"Do you think that's appropriate?" Emily's mother asked. "Rang her bell?"

Dr. S turned back to Emily. "Does your bell feel like it's

been rung?"

Emily smiled. Even without looking at her mother, Emily knew she was mad.

"I think it would be best if when you go out again, you have the nurse clamp off your IV so you don't have all that tubing and the IV pole. Less chance of tripping," Dr. S said.

"There won't be a next time," Emily's mother said.

"Mom."

"You're sick enough. We don't need you out there falling over and hurting yourself."

"I'm sure with the right supervision, Emily will be okay," Dr. S said.

"No, she's not going out there again."

Dr. S and Emily's mother stared at each other for a long moment until Dr. S turned to Emily. "Suzy Q, you've had quite a long day. Close your eyes and get some rest now."

Rosa

Rosa re-traced the lines of the hopscotch board while Mike, her cameraman, set up for the shoot. After talking with Janice in PR again, they'd decided they would start with a short news segment, see what sort of reactions they got, and maybe do a follow up in a week or so.

Ray stood off to the side of the cameraman. Rosa had told him the night before that she'd be reporting on the hopscotch board first thing in the morning. When she asked if he could be there, he said he wouldn't miss it for the world.

Rosa winked at Ray and smiled at the camera as Mike raised his right hand indicating they were almost ready. As the camera's green light flashed on, Rosa began speaking into the microphone: "Here at Alfred Stone Memorial Hospital in Greensboro where patients are treated and healed, a children's game is breathing fresh life into the hospital and lifting the spirits of everyone who comes in contact with it."

As the cameraman started filming a couple of visitors on the hopscotch board, Rosa noticed that blond girl's father sitting alone, on a bench twenty feet away. She turned to Ray. "Isn't that Emily's father? Could you introduce us?"

Ray nodded, then waved Clay Andrews over. The man walked toward them slowly. "Hi, Dr. Hernandez," he said.

"Rosa, this is Clay Andrews," Ray said. "Mr. Andrews, this is my wife, Rosa. I've got to run."

"Can I talk to you for a minute?" Rosa asked.

"Sure," Mr. Andrews said.

Ray went back inside to check on his patients as Rosa and Mr. Andrews walked toward the picnic bench where she'd sat and watched Emily and that little girl play. Rosa told him how inspiring his daughter had been, and seeing her out here had touched her and that she'd really like to include her in the news report.

"I don't know," he said. "We're private people and this has been hard enough on Emily and her mother."

"I think your little girl is an inspiration," Rosa said.

Mr. Andrews looked beyond Rosa's right shoulder as if something in the trees had caught his attention. But she saw his lip start to tremble, the tears, and then he lowered his head into his hand.

"It's okay," Rosa said. And she said it again.

He wiped his sleeve. "I've gotta get back upstairs for when she wakes up."

It began to snow. The first snow of the year, fat white

flakes hitting the picnic bench and their hair and faces. They both smiled. Clay opened his mouth and stuck his tongue out to taste the snow, but it didn't taste like anything at all.

She handed him her business card, said, "Call me if you change your mind. I think she'll be inspiring to other kids and I think it will be good for her. What kid wouldn't want to see themselves on TV?"

He didn't say anything but slid the card in his pocket.

Rosa told her cameraman they'd better pack it up for today. They'll have to come back in a couple days to get more shots of people on the board.

Clay Andrews

When Clay walked back in Emily's room, Bev turned away from the window. "What did she want?"

"They're doing a report on that hopscotch board. Apparently, nobody knows where it came from. It's some sort of Christmas mystery. The reporter said she wanted to include Emily in the news report."

"No," Bev said.

"But Mom," Emily said. "I want to."

Her parents looked at each other. They'd both thought she was sleeping.

"We're not going to take another chance on you falling and getting hurt," her mother said.

"Emily," her father said. "Come over to the window and see the snow."

"I don't care about stupid snow," Emily said.

Clay turned to Bev. "Happy now?"

He walked out of the room. He didn't know where he

was going, but for a few minutes he needed to get away from his wife, Bev, and her damn negative attitude. And he needed to somehow try and make Emily feel better. As a mechanic, he was used to people bringing him cars that didn't work and he would fix them. But he could not fix his little girl.

He wiped his eyes as he settled behind the seat of his old Ford Ranger. He pulled out of the lot and drove with no destination in mind. He needed to see something besides the four walls of that damn hospital room. He drove through the light snow. For some reason he couldn't explain, Clay found the snow, and his windshield wipers clicking back and forth, oddly comforting and peaceful.

At the first stop light, Clay saw a man he recognized from the hospital, a man on the housekeeping crew he'd seen a few times. His navy blue jacket was covered with snow. Clay rolled his window down. "Need a ride?"

The man looked over at him suspiciously.

"My daughter's a patient at the hospital. I've seen you there," Clay said.

As the man recognized him, his face relaxed. He opened the door, climbed in, and extended his hand. "John Deaver," he said.

"Clay Andrews."

"Yeah, I've seen you and your daughter at the hospital."

Clay laughed. "It seems like everyone has."

"I only live a couple miles out on Elm Street."

"It's no problem," Clay said.

"Your girl sure likes to jump on that hopscotch board."

"She loves it," Clay said. "What about you, John? Do you have any children?"

"I do. Her name's Shanna," John said. As the words left his mouth, John was surprised at himself. Whenever someone asked if he had children, he usually said no. It was easier than explaining how he'd lost her and what had happened with Tara. "She's a senior this year."

Clay knew it would take a miracle for Emily to make it to seventeen or eighteen. "I hope you guys have a great holiday season."

"Thanks, Clay. And I hope your little girl gets to go home for Christmas."

"Me too," Clay said. "Me too."

After dropping John off, Clay drove past their house and the park where he had walked with Emily so many times. Even back when she was a baby and he'd pushed her in a stroller. He drove by her school, and finally stopped at a toy store. He followed the worn path in the snow up the sidewalk to the store's entrance.

As soon as Clay walked in the store, he knew he'd made a mistake. Every kid he saw was happy, healthy, running around and laughing with their parents. Doing what kids were supposed to do. He'd gone in to buy something to make Emily happy, but the only thing that had made her truly happy lately was her time out on the hopscotch board. But now with her fall, he doubted he'd be able to convince Bev to let her go out there again. Plus, with the weather turning colder and the snow it didn't look like the hopscotch board would even be out there much longer.

At the register, he spotted a plastic box of sidewalk chalk. The blues and reds and yellows. He bought three boxes of sidewalk chalk and headed back to his family.

Metalhead Mike

Metalhead watches the snowfall, covering the trees and sidewalk. He thinks he likes snow, but doesn't know. He can't remember ever sledding or making a snowman or having a snowball fight with his parents or the friends he must have had.

He climbs under the sheets and tries to remember snow, what it's like to have your whole yard covered in white, but instead he's at the kitchen table, playing some handheld videogame, and his mother is at the stove, moving a pan this way and that, reaching into the refrigerator for ingredients. He's not sure what she's cooking. It's the middle of the day and he's still wearing his bathing suit. They've just returned home from a morning at the pool, and he can still see her blue suit under the long white shirt she wears.

But he's not really paying attention to her because he's working his game, thumb thumping on a tiny square of a screen and some characters he can't quite see.

"Iced tea?" she asks. And when he doesn't respond she says it again, louder, "Iced tea?"

He says sure though she probably could have asked him if he wanted a cup of gasoline and he'd have said sure. He's not paying attention. It seems in his memory he's never paying attention to what's in front of him. She sets the glass of tea down on the table. There's lots of ice in the tea, but he knows there's no sugar in there. Still, the tea tastes good and cold. His mother sets a pair of plates on the table, each has a neat stack of Pringles and a grilled cheese sandwich with gooey yellow cheese leaking out the sides.

His mother says, "Put the game away, Mike."

She always makes him put the game away when they're eating. On those rare meals when his mother is not home, his father doesn't make him turn off the game while they eat.

His mother says, "You weren't very nice to Ben today."

"We were just playing," he says. "We push people in the pool all the time."

"He didn't seem too happy."

"He's done it to me before."

She takes a couple bites of her grilled cheese, washes it down with some tea. "Be nice to people, Mike," she says.

"I am."

"Today, you weren't. Just be nice to people."

He knows she's right. He knows he pushed a little too hard, and the reason he did it was because Ben had pushed him in the day before when he wasn't ready.

"Good grilled cheese," he says.

She smiles at him, because she knows he's trying to change the subject. She tells him they have to go to the grocery store this afternoon and he says sure, whatever she wants to do. It's summer, long fun days without school. And so they eat their grilled cheese sandwiches; the only sound is the ice in their glasses, a car outside, his mother's cell phone ringing, her winking at him and saying, "It can wait. Whoever it is, it can wait."

John

Back in his apartment, John ate a handful of peanut butter crackers. He'd enjoyed talking with Clay. He seemed like a decent man. It was a shame how sick his daughter was. And thinking about that little girl and her father, made John want to see Shanna even more.

He wanted to stand a few feet away from her at that Hardees counter and see her smile up at him. But John knew there were things he could and could not do. If he went to her Hardees more than once a week, she might recognize him and get suspicious and tell someone. Maybe she would recognize him and say Daddy and they would run off together, move to another town and start a new life. But he knew this was a dream and for now he should be happy with what they had—a weekly meeting of strangers. Once she turned eighteen, in ten months, he would contact her.

He remembered sitting with Shanna on their old tan couch, watching that purple dinosaur Barney, and he remembered a show where Barney played hopscotch. Shanna had stood up in their living room, jumping on their white carpet, following Barney's instructions. But Shanna was not a little girl anymore and that house and his old life were gone now.

John took a shower and listened to his favorite CD, *Kind of Blue* by Miles Davis, while he changed into shorts and a T-shirt. The bedroom light was not on and John started to hop across the dark room as if there was a hopscotch board there. He knew the bed was on one side of the room, his dresser on the other. He closed his eyes and jumped until he reached the wall and then he turned and hopped all the way back to the other side.

When he finally fell into his bed, the CD had stopped and there was a layer of sweat across his body. He closed his eyes but sleep would not come easy. He could feel his heart thumping from all the hopping. He could see Shanna standing beside his bed in the hospital room, asking about her mother. And John not being able to say anything besides *I'm sorry, baby, I'm sorry.* Shanna walked away with his father-in-law and never returned to his side again.

Emily

Emily opened her eyes and saw her mother walk over to the small Christmas tree in the corner of her room. She pulled a bag of purple beads and a candy bar from her coat pocket and glanced back at Emily once, then slid the gifts under the tree. Emily thought it was too dark for her mother to realize she wasn't actually sleeping. She stayed perfectly still and had no intention of letting her mother know she was excited about whatever she'd placed under the tree.

She hoped it was a Milky Way bar, her favorite. She considered opening her eyes and saying, "I caught you, Mom," but she was still mad at her mother for saying she wouldn't be able to go outside to the hopscotch board again.

Each morning the gifts would be there under the tree, and Emily knew it was always her mother that gave them to her. She never pretended they were from Santa Claus, only shrugged her shoulders whenever Emily asked who they were from.

As her mother sat in the chair, a few feet away, Emily closed her eyes tighter. She would not wake up just yet. She'd prefer to wait until her mother was gone, then she could walk over to the tree and act surprised at the sight of these new gifts.

John

Although it was a Saturday, John came into work to clear the snow from the hopscotch board. While it had snowed three inches, only an inch or so stuck to the ground. Someone had cleared a clean path from the parking lot to the hospital entrance, but they hadn't cleared the area with the hopscotch board. In fact, they'd piled some of the snow up there, which is what John had guessed would happen.

The weatherman said it might make it into the low 50's, so the snow would probably all melt away by the end of the day, but he wanted and needed to do something. John took his jacket off and began to shovel the sidewalk and the area where the board had been. When he'd shoveled all the snow away, tossing it into the leaves and grass that bordered the sidewalk and walkway, he went inside the hospital and grabbed a couple of the fans they used to dry the floors after waxing. Waiting for the sidewalk to dry, he sat on the bench, breathing in that cool December air.

"John, what are you doing?"

John looked up. It was Bruce, the weekend supervisor.

"Just cleaning off the sidewalks."

Bruce, a tall man with a crew cut, shook his head. He was standing just to the side of the large fans. "You can't be out here working on your day off, John."

Some people thought Bruce was a tough boss, but he'd been decent to John, even back when he'd first started working here. John said, "I've got to clean these sidewalks for the kids who want to play hopscotch."

Bruce shook his head. "Hopscotch?"

"Someone drew a hopscotch board on the sidewalk and the patients like it. The kids come out here and use the thing."

"I'll get one of the weekend guys to do it. Go home, spend time with your family."

"I've got nothing to go home to," John said.

Bruce sighed as if only then remembering John's story, the accident and everything that came after. "Alright, but don't go and throw your back out. That's all we need."

"I'm just sitting on a bench, watching the ground dry."

Bruce smiled and said, "You're a good man, John Deaver."

"I wish," John said.

"Leave the fans out here. Don't you dare try to carry them back inside. I'll send one of the guys out here in a couple hours to collect them." Bruce picked up the broom and shovel, as if to make sure John wouldn't be able to use them anymore.

"Fine, Bruce. Fine."

After he was gone, John squeezed his hands in his jeans pocket, as if to push the cold away. When he looked up at the hospital, he spotted that little blond girl, her hand against the window. John smiled and waved. She waved back, then stepped away from the window.

A few more minutes you little angel, he thought, just a few more minutes.

Emily

Emily stepped back from the window and turned to her mother. "That man just cleared the snow off the sidewalk. Can't we go out there, please?"

"I've already told you," her mother said. "You're done with that. You could fall and get hurt. Plus, it's getting too cold. If you want to play hopscotch, you can do it here in the room or even go to the playroom down the hall."

"Mom," she said. "It's not the same."

"It's for your own good."

"But Mom," Emily said. "I want to go outside again."

"We can go for a walk, but you're not going to go out there and jump on that hopscotch board again. I didn't want you to do it in the first place, but I let you and you got hurt."

"You're a mean jerk," Emily said.

Her mother turned to her. In an instant, her face changed from mad to hurt. Emily wished she hadn't said it, but she couldn't take it back. Her mother walked out of the room.

Emily considered going after her, apologizing. She knew her mother wasn't mean, not really. She was just trying to protect her, but Emily didn't want to be protected. She just wanted to go outside and do something she liked to do before it was too late.

Yes, her knee and elbow were both still a little sore from the fall, but she didn't care. What's the worst thing that could happen? She could fall and break her neck? So what.

Emily decided to sneak past the nurse's station and make a run for the board. That man had come and cleared off the snow, had drawn a new board for her. Of course, it wasn't only for Emily, but to her it felt like it was.

After easing on her jacket, she held onto her IV pole and opened the door. So far so good. Juliet, her nurse, smiled at her but didn't say anything. She didn't see her parents anywhere. That chunky boy with the scar on his head was walking with a therapist, his hands out in front of him. Emily assumed they were working on balance or something, but she thought with his hands out like that, and the scar of his head, it made him sort of look like a zombie.

She asked Glennis, the unit secretary, to unlock the door so she could leave. Glennis was a short, thick woman from England. She had a strong English accent. "Where are you going, Miss Emily?"

"I'm going to meet my Mom in the gift shop," Emily said.

Glennis turned back to Juliet, as if to say what do you think. Juliet nodded it would be okay, so Glennis pushed the button under the counter to unlock the door.

Emily almost laughed out loud, amazed at how easy it was to get out. But beside the time she got mad and ran last week she hadn't done anything to make them suspicious. She could feel a pin prick of pain in her knee with each step she took, but told herself to forget about that for now. She could breathe a little easier outside of that room. There was the elevator, up ahead. She pushed the down arrow and waited, half-expecting Glennis or Juliet to call her back.

When the elevator door opened, her mother and father were standing there, holding cups of coffee. Both of their eyes opened wide as they saw her. "And where exactly are you going?" her mother asked.

"For a walk."

"No, you are not," her mother said, handing her coffee cup to Emily's dad. She grabbed Emily's arm and led her back to her room.

"Dad," Emily said. "Don't let her do this to me."

"Oh, Emily, knock off the drama," her mother said.

Her father didn't say anything, only walked ahead of them and opened the door. In the room, Emily tore off her jacket so fast she pulled the IV out of her arm again. It stung and started bleeding. "Now look what you've done again," her mom said. She went off to get the nurse to put in a new line as Emily climbed back into bed.

When they were alone, Emily turned to her father, who was holding some gauze to her arm. "I can't believe you won't stick up for me."

"I think that's enough out of you," her father said. "We will jump on that hopscotch board again, but you can't go sneaking off. Do you understand me? You're driving your mother crazy."

Her father didn't usually get mad at her, so Emily knew she'd probably gone too far. But she didn't care. Not today, not now. Plus, he had said that they would play hopscotch outside again.

"Fine," she said. She picked up her DS and played her Mario Brothers game. She squeezed the game and pushed the buttons down so hard she thought she might break it, but she didn't. When her mother returned, she didn't say anything, but sat in one of the chairs beside the table and closed her eyes, rubbed her forehead, as if she had a terrible headache.

But her mother had her where she wanted her: in her soft bed where she was safe from that mean old hopscotch board that wanted to hurt her. Emily shook her head and stared at the tiny game in her hands. God, she hated her mother. She stared so hard she could no longer focus and the screen turned into colors instead of tiny characters and the colors turned into nothing and it was as if the game in her hand wasn't even there.

Mary

When Mary pulled into the hospital's parking lot, her two grandsons, Mitch and Blake, asked why they were here. "I want to show you something," Mary said. She'd told Rosemarie, her oldest daughter, she wanted to take the boys for a drive to talk about their grandfather and to maybe pick out some Christmas gifts. While that was partly true, she'd planned all along to stop by the hospital hopscotch board.

The boys were five and seven, and lived in Iowa, so Mary knew she wouldn't have another opportunity to show them this.

They had been stoic at Walter's funeral, in their Sunday best outifts: pants and bow ties and black shoes. She wished Walter had been able to see them today. And perhaps, she thought, he had.

She took each by the hand and they walked toward the entrance. "When your grandfather and I were young, back before we were married, he proposed to me while playing hopscotch. Do you boys know how to play hopscotch?"

"Of course," Mitch said.

Blake reached for his bow tie and said, "It's more of a girl game at my school. Boys don't usually play hopscotch."

Mary smiled. "We'll see about that."

When they reached the board, one of the hospital janitor's was sweeping off what remained of the snow from the sidewalk. He tipped his hat to Mary and the boys.

Without her having to say anything, the boys walked over to the board and each selected a stone. In the grass, there were a few softball-sized patches of snow, but really any evidence of yesterday's snow was completely gone.

Blake turned to his grandmother and said, "Grandma, aren't you going to play?"

Mary felt her face flash hot and knew she was about to cry. It hadn't occurred to her to actually play with them. But why not?

Blake handed her a purple stone and said she should go first. Mary tossed the stone and it landed in the number 1 box, so she hopped there. Her legs felt good; her heart strong and full. When she looked back at the boys they were smiling at her.

Hours earlier, she had buried her husband. And now she was here with her grandchildren, playing hopscotch. Her heart filled with something as light and peaceful as joy, and she tried not to cry. She would no doubt miss Walter often in the days and weeks to come. But for now she had her grandchildren around her and she was playing hopscotch here and she felt pretty good. She told herself to hold on to that feeling for as long as she could.

After playing, they would stop by Tim's Tike's Toys at the shopping center by Mary's house and she'd let each boy pick out a gift and of course they would be happy about this, but she believed they were happy to be here playing with her. The real purpose of Christmas, she thought, is to be with your family. And while she wished Walter was here, she had her grandchildren and her grown children were back at the house, waiting for her, for them, where they'd all be together for a little while longer.

Emily

Emily sat up when there was a knock at her door. She hoped it wasn't time for one of her treatments. Her mother was in the corner, reading a magazine. When the door opened, it wasn't her nurse, or even Dr. S, but instead Santa Claus himself.

"Ho-ho-ho," he bellowed.

He was a skinny Santa with black-framed glasses instead of the usual big-bellied, wire-rimmed-glasses version. And he looked a little too young to be Santa, but Emily smiled nonetheless. Her mother stood as if she were about to position herself between Emily and this Santa.

"This must be the one and only Emily Andrews," Santa said.

"That's me."

"I wanted to come by and see what you wanted for Christmas."

Emily noticed her mother was staring at her father who had walked in behind Santa. Her father smiled at Emily, but didn't look over at her mother.

Santa sat in the chair next to the bed and leaned against the rail there. Emily squeezed his white-gloved hand in hers. "Well," she said. "I'd like to be out of the hospital, so I can decorate my Christmas tree at home. I'd like to run around in my backyard and ride my bike and see my friends."

Santa smiled, patting her hand. "Would you like any videogames or dolls? Maybe a Barbie?"

Emily shrugged her shoulders. "I've already got those things." She looked over at her mother, who had her hands folded across her chest. "I'd also really like to go outside and jump on the hopscotch board again. And maybe even have my friends, Holly and her brother Luke, come and jump with me."

Santa turned to her father, as if to try and understand a little of what she was asking for. "Hopscotch, huh?"

Clay nodded. "Someone drew a hopscotch board out

on the sidewalk and Emily likes to go out there and play, but a couple days days ago she fell and we think . . ." He paused and looked over at Bev.

Bev stepped forward. "We think it's too dangerous. She might get hurt, and she's gone through so much already."

"Well, what did the doctors say?" Santa asked.

"They said it would be okay," Emily said.

"It is Christmas, Mom," Santa said. "And if Emily wants to play hopscotch, and her doctors say it's okay, then I say let's go play a game. I haven't played in years."

"It's not up to you," Bev said.

Santa smiled. "I guess you're right. It's not."

Emily's mother said, "Clay, did you put him up to this?"

Santa said, "Who's Clay?"

Clay shook his head. "No, I didn't. He was visiting all the kid's rooms and I told him to make sure he came to see Emily. That's it."

Her mother turned to Santa, who nodded as he helped Emily slide her jacket on over her new IV.

Her father said, "We'll be right there, Bev. We'll catch her if we need to. And how many kids get to play hopscotch with Santa Claus?"

"Fine," Bev said, throwing her hands in the air as if she wanted to grab everyone in this room and shake them until they understood what she wanted, what she knew was best for her daughter. She pushed open the door and walked away from them, down the hall.

Santa looked at Clay as if he was giving it a second thought, but Emily was not going to let this chance pass by. She already had hold of her IV pole and was heading for the door.

As promised, Clay stood on one side of her while Santa

stood on the other. Emily may not have jumped as hard as she had a couple days earlier, but still she jumped and hopped and breathed in the cold, light air. After a few minutes, she looked up and saw her mother standing at the entrance to the hospital, her arms still tight against her chest as if protecting herself from the cold or from all of this, something she could not control.

Emily waved and her mother lifted her hand to wave back, as if finally giving in, before walking toward them. She sat on the bench and watched Emily and Clay and Santa do what they'd come outside to do. Emily thought her mother had given her the best Christmas gift ever.

Metalhead Mike

Metalhead walks over to the window. With the trees bare, he can see the large black building across Maple Street, the cars passing by on the street below. But when he looks down, there's a man in a red suit, jumping on the hopscotch board. Is it really Santa Claus? Metalhead blinks twice and still Santa Claus is down on the sidewalk, hopping. Metalhead can't help but think of last Christmas.

He drinks hot chocolate while his parents drink their coffee and his father eats the half-cookie Santa hadn't finished. The presents are laid out under the tree and while he can't remember everything his parents have given him he remembers games and a couple new books. Metalhead wonders if he's the sort of kid who likes to read. When he's tried now, the tiny words on the page give him headaches. He's sitting between his parents, watching the Charlie Brown Christmas special. Of course, he's seen it a bunch of times before but his parents want to watch it with him. Snoopy is his favorite. He remembers the warmth of being surrounded by them, and the desire to get up and grab his new game and go off into his room and play.

For a moment, at the hospital window, Metalhead feels his parents standing on either side of him. He can smell something that may have been his mother's perfume or his father's cigarettes. When he turns to look, there's no one there, only an empty room.

He wipes the tears away. Santa Claus is still outside, hopping with a small person Metalhead thinks at first it might be an elf but then realizes it's that blond girl. And suddenly, Metalhead knows he has to go outside and see Santa. Something tells him if he sees Santa everything will be all right. It'll be Christmas again, like last year, and his parents will be with him watching that old Charlie Brown Christmas special.

He heads for the elevator and jumps in behind a man he thinks must be someone's father. He can hear Glennis, the secretary, yell his name as the elevator door closes.

"You supposed to be leaving?" the man asks.

"Are you?" Metalhead asks.

Before the man can answer, the door opens and Metalhead runs by him. In the lobby, he passes that blond girl and her parents walking back toward the elevator. He walks as fast as he can. He still hasn't quite regained all his balance. When he makes it outside the cold air hits him quick, takes his breath, but he doesn't care. He looks around, but there's no Santa, only an empty hopscotch board. He can't breathe. His head hurts. His eyes and lips sting. He sits on the bench and buries his head in his arms. He wants to scream, wants to punch something, anything, so he punches his thighs and the bench he's sitting on and the air all around him.

When he tires of this, and catches his breath, he stands and walks toward the board. He positions his feet in the starting box, but he can't move. It's like the hopscotch board is made of quickstand and is sucking him in. Something is missing. There is no other way to explain all this. He knows he's supposed to jump, but for some reason he can't. It's as if the message from his brain to his knees, saying jump, dammit, jump, doesn't quite work.

"You okay, son?"

Metalhead looks up. Santa Claus is standing a few feet away with a red coat so bright it's almost blinding. Metalhead turns and hugs him, feels the soft, wool tickling his face.

"All right, all right, my boy. It's okay."

Metalhead continues to hug him as his crying slows.

"Mike."

Metalhead turns and his nurse, Helen, is standing at the door, looking none too happy about his escape. But her face seems to soften a little as she takes in Santa, the hug, and what made the boy run. "Come on, Mike. Let's get you back upstairs."

"In a minute," he says. "Santa, aren't you supposed to ask me what I want for Christmas?"

Santa looks over his head, toward Helen. He clears his throat. "Haven't had time, young man. I was on my way back upstairs to do just that. So what do you want for Christmas?"

"I want my parents' back. I want my old house. I want to sit at my kitchen table while my mom makes me grilled cheese. I want to watch TV with my dad."

"Well," Santa said. "That's quite a bit."

Helen walks over toward Mike and Santa and without a

word the three of them are hugging there on the sidewalk.

She says, "Oh, Mike."

"I know you can't give me all that," Metalhead says. "They're gone, and you're not really Santa Claus, but I wonder if maybe you could just hop with me like you were with that girl."

"I think we can do that," Santa says.

Santa holds one of his hands, while Helen holds the other. They hop together, the three of them, from one to ten and back again. They stop a couple times to rest and sometimes where there's one block, Metalhead lands with two feet, but still they do finish the whole board.

Santa hugs Metalhead again, wishes him a Merry Christmas and tells Helen he'll be back up on the floor in a few minutes to see the rest of the kids. Helen walks Metalhead back to his room where he slides under the sheets, his feet only now beginning to warm up. He closes his eyes and tries his best not to play the Memory Game. For a few minutes, he doesn't want to remember anything before today. He's just jumped and hopped with Santa Claus, and he wants to hold on to that for as long as he can before it too slips away into nothing more than the past.

Rosa

When Rosa received the call from Emily Andrews's father, saying she could do the interview now if she was still interested, Rosa cancelled three appointments and called her camerman and told him to meet her at the hospital ASAP.

For the last two days, Rosa had driven out to the hospital

to see if people were still using the hopscotch board. And they were—from patients to visitors and staff. She'd even seen Santa hopping with some kids.

In the middle of the day, when it was warmest, no more than ten minutes ever passed before someone hopped on the board. Most people didn't do the whole thing, but would hop one or two boxes and go on from there, either entering the hospital or heading to the parking deck.

Rosa smiled at Glennis, the unit secretary, and walked on toward Emily's room. She took a deep breath and knocked.

"Come in." Rosa recognized Mr. Andrews' voice.

She pushed the door open and the girl was sitting on her bed, the sheets pulled up past her knees. Emily had a small plastic box full of tiny colorful beads, and she was sliding red and yellow beads onto a thin wire bracelet. She smiled as she looked up at Rosa.

"Mrs. Hernandez," Emily said.

"Call me Rosa."

"Rosa," Emily said and smiled.

The room was decorated like a kid's room with stuffed animals, a Dora the Explorer doll, some flowers and even a poster of a pair of twin boys Rosa didn't recognize. They were both holding guitars and wearing thin ties. The door to the bathroom was bordered by colorful tinsel and a miniature Christmas tree sat on the end table. But on the other side of the room was the oxygen tank, the overflowing garbage can, and boxes of gloves and clean sheets, to remind you this was not a typical kid's bedroom.

"Did your dad tell you I wanted to videotape you playing on the hopscotch board, maybe even interview you?"

Emily's eyes brightened as she nodded. The door

opened and Emily's mom walked in. She looked tired and in need of a haircut. Rosa wondered what she looked like years ago before Emily got sick. She knew from some of the stories she'd done what grief could do to people, how it could eat them up. She tried to imagine Mrs. Andrews back when Emily was still a baby and her life was hopeful and stretched out before her like any other child.

"Bev, this is Rosa," Mr. Andrews said.

She looked back at Rosa. "Hi."

Rosa wished she could take this mother and hug her, squeeze the bitterness right out of her. But how would Rosa herself respond, if she was given a beautiful child like Emily, only to be told she would be losing her much too early?

"Can I talk to you outside?" Mrs. Andrews asked Rosa.

"Of course," Rosa said, following her out the door.

In the hall, Mrs. Andrews said, "Why are you doing this?"

"I think Emily is special. I think other kids will watch her and be inspired by her."

Mrs. Andrews shook her head. "We shouldn't be here. Emily should be in school and I should be volunteering on the PTA, helping her class with activities."

"I know," Rosa said. She lifted her arms to hug Mrs. Andrews, but the woman turned and walked back inside the room.

Rosa sat down at the nursing station and dried her own eyes with tissue. Juliet smiled at her. "She'll be okay."

Mike, the cameraman, called Rosa's cell and said he was pulling into the parking lot and should be ready in five minutes. As she hung up, Rosa heard someone coughing and looked up. A little boy in a wheelchair was being pushed by his mother. He was thin and blonde with the softest blue eyes she had ever seen. His mother pushed him right up to Rosa.

He sat up in the chair and waved. "Can I have your autograph?"

Rosa smiled. "Only if I can have yours."

He laughed.

"So what's your name?" Rosa asked.

"Garrett. Garrett Jacobs."

"It's nice to meet you," Rosa said. She shook his hand and then his mother's. She was tall and athletic looking. She did not look like the sort of person who spent much time in hospitals.

"He watches you on TV all the time," Garrett's mom said.

"Now why would you want to do that when there's all those cool cartoons to watch?" Rosa asked playfully.

"Because you're pretty," he said, blushing as he said it.

Rosa smiled and hugged him.

"Is Dr. Ray really your husband?" Garrett asked.

"Yes, it's true."

Garrett looked up at his mom and smiled. "I knew it," he said. "Is that why you're here?"

She shook her head. "Have you seen that hopscotch board outside?"

"No," he said. It occurred to Rosa for the first time that the rooms on the opposite side of the hall didn't face the sidewalk and the patients there wouldn't see the hopscotch board from their windows.

"I'm doing a report on this hopscotch board outside. Nobody knows where it came from."

"Can I come with you?" Garrett asked.

"Sure, you can."

Garrett turned to his mother and said, "Can we get

Metalhead Mike?"

His mother nodded. "I told you not to call him that."

"That's what he calls himself."

Garrett climbed out of the wheelchair and walked to a room on the far side of the hall. Apparently, he hadn't needed the wheelchair after all.

"Metalhead Mike?" Rosa asked.

Garrett's mom shook her head. "He was in a car accident and fractured his skull so they screwed it back together with a couple metal plates."

"If you don't mind me asking, Mrs. Jacobs, why is Garrett in the hospital?"

"Leukemia. The doctors say he might be okay. The best they can give us is might."

"I'm sorry," Rosa said.

"Don't be. Might is better than nothing. And don't ask Mike about his parents. They were both killed in the car wreck. I don't think he knows."

"My God," Rosa said.

Metalhead Mike looked like any other chunky ten year old kid except for the shaved head and comma-shaped scar above his left ear. She could see a couple indentions in his skin from the metal plates. He also had a cast on his right forearm and was missing a couple of his front teeth. He was a mess.

"Wow," Mike said. "You're hot."

Rosa smiled. "Why thank you, Mike. You're quite the gentleman."

"Call me Metalhead," he said.

When he stuck his hand out to shake, Rosa hugged him instead. It occurred to her she'd hugged more people today than she had in the last week.

She felt a twinge of guilt that she hadn't visited the

floor in almost three months. She used to come once a week, then once a month, cheering up the kids by reading them stories. She had stopped, saying she was too busy, letting one of the new reporters do it instead. While she hated to admit it, the real reason she had stopped coming was because it had broken her heart to see all of these sick children.

As Garrett walked up, Rosa opened her arms and the three of them hugged.

"Let me in on this." They all looked up as Ray ran toward them, opened armed and smiling. And he too was part of the hug.

Emily's door opened and she came out with her parents, each one on either side of her. She wore jeans under her hospital gown and that same pink parka along with brown Uggs. Her mother had combed her hair, pulled what she could back into a ponytail. Rosa thought she looked strong and beautiful.

After Rosa introduced Emily to the two boys, she asked her if they could come down to the board with them.

"Of course," Emily said. "I'll enjoy beating them."

"We'll see about that," Metalhead Mike said.

Emily

Emily didn't mind sharing Rosa with the other kids. She'd seen the blonde boy and the boy with the shaved head playing on the Wii in the game room a couple times but had never really talked to either one of them. The blonde boy was cute and his mother was tall and blonde and Emily thought she looked like a model.

Outside, the cold wind surprised her for a moment, made her eyes water. There was a man at one end of the hopscotch board with a big video camera. Rosa told her to just hop back and forth a few times so he could get some video of her playing. While her father and Rosa had told her she would be on TV, Emily still didn't believe it.

After Emily hopped the distance of the board twice, she sat next to Rosa on the bench. Rosa asked her a few questions with the cameraman filming them. She said it was an interview, but to Emily it felt like she was chatting with a friend. The questions were about the hopscotch board, when she first saw it, why she liked coming outside and playing on the board.

"I saw these two men," Emily said. "One was in a wheelchair and the other one was jumping for him. Nobody believed me at first, but then Dad saw them too. I hadn't played hopscotch in at least a year, but when I saw this one I knew I had to play. So Mom and Dad and me came down here and played and the funny thing is that if I close my eyes and pretend I'm not wearing a hospital gown with a mask on my face, it feels like I'm back at Brooks Global, my school, jumping on the playground with Mrs. Courtland, our PE teacher, cheering me on."

Emily looked up at Rosa and saw the tears in her eyes. It hadn't occurred to Emily that this would be a sad story. Rosa wiped her eyes and turned to the camera, with Emily leaning on her shoulder, and said, "Here at the entrance to Alfred Stone Memorial Hospital in Greensboro, something as simple as a child's game is making a difference in people's lives." She paused a moment, then said, "Cut. That'll do it, Mike."

After Rosa helped Mike load his equipment into the News2 van, she stayed and played with Emily and the two boys.

They had to explain the rules to Metalhead Mike a few times. Emily thought it was weird a kid his age wouldn't know how to play hopscotch, but he said that particular memory must have gotten bounced out of his head in the accident. Maybe it drifted into the air when they had his skull cracked open in surgery. He didn't seem to mind talking about his surgery.

Emily looked over and saw her mother talking to Garrett's mom. Since she'd gotten sick, her mom had stopped hanging out with her friends. She'd stopped going to her Tuesday night bowling league. She seemed, Emily thought, to have stopped living.

Emily used to love those Tuesday nights. Not because her mother was gone, but because her dad would sit next to her on the couch reading a thick, paperback novel while she watched Cartoon Network or Nickelodeon and when they'd see her mom's car pull into the driveway they'd run into the kitchen where her dad would start the dishes and she would pretend she'd been working on her homework. Her dad would turn to her and wink as her mom walked in the door.

Emily was tired of thinking about before and after and tried to concentrate on this game. Garrett was pretty good at hopscotch, but on every third or fourth jump Metalhead Mike would practically fall over. Emily's dad stood beside Metalhead and held his arm for balance. Then it was just Emily and Garrett playing, because Metalhead Mike and Emily's dad started talking about something else and walked over to the picnic table.

Emily won the first match, but Garrett had won the second, so they had to do a tie-breaker. Emily was starting to get tired, but Garrett seemed to be getting stronger and better the longer they played.

"Hey kids."

When Emily turned around, she saw Rosa walking toward her and Garrett with another girl. Emily had seen her on the floor before—short and redheaded, with an arm that seemed attached to her side. And she limped real bad, sort of like she was dragging one of her legs when she walked. When Emily had seen her on the hospital unit the girl was always walking around with one of those physical therapists.

"Emily and Garrett," Rosa said. "This is Beth. Can she play with you?"

"Sure," Emily said, relieved she wouldn't have to finish the tie-breaker match with Garrett.

Emily wasn't expecting much because of the limp and the arm but the girl could actually hop just fine even if it looked a little awkward. And she smiled an awful lot, like she was surprised and delighted to be outside with them.

"What are you in for?" Garrett asked.

In for, Emily thought, she's not in prison, you silly boy.

"I have to have surgery on my arm to see if they can get my fingers straighter," Beth said. With her other hand, she pried her fingers apart and splayed them out, so that they almost looked normal.

Metalhead Mike

Metalhead Mike doesn't know what they're talking about. He can't remember the exact rules for playing hopscotch even if Miss Fancy Pants, Emily, says he must have played it in school. When he was out here with Santa the other day, they just hopped, from one box to the next.

They didn't throw any stones or play by any rules or anything like that. This Emily girl and her rules are starting to give him a headache.

He'd like to think he was an athlete before the accident. That he was good at baseball or basketball, maybe even football, but the truth is he just doesn't know.

It's like the wires in his brain that should remember this, and everything else, have been disconnected. He wants to throw himself at a wall or punch something, hoping it will somehow snap him out of this, perhaps jar everything in his brain back to normal. But he's not even sure what normal is anymore.

Maybe it's the medicine. Maybe that's what is keeping him in a fog, a fog he is not able to swim through no matter how hard he tries, over and over again.

When Emily's father walks up to him and asks if he wants to arm wrestle, Metalhead Mike says *heck yeah*. It seems odd to be asked to arm wrestle, but no odder than playing hopscotch on the sidewalk with a TV film crew. Or even jumping around in a bunch of boxes with Santa Claus.

As they walk away from the crowd at the hopscotch board, over toward the picnic table, Metalhead asks why he wants to arm wrestle.

"Because you look more like an arm wrestler than a hopscotcher to me," he says.

"You got that right," Metalhead says. "What's your name?"

"Clay. What's yours?"

"Mike. You can call me Metalhead Mike."

"That's a strange name," Clay says.

Metalhead Mike touches his head in response. Metalhead and Emily's dad sit on opposite sides of the picnic bench.

"I used to be the Gaston County Arm Wrestling Champion," Clay Andrews says.

Metalhead doesn't buy this. He knows there's a world he doesn't understand, but this man don't look like a champion arm wrestler. He doesn't look like a champion anything, just a guy with a sick daughter, sad eyes and baggy jeans. He looks, Metalhead thinks, like a man whose about to get beat at arm wrestling by a ten-year-old brain damaged boy.

They grip hands. Metalhead notices the man's hands are calloused and his knuckles are big, so this might be more of a challenge than he expected. So he grips tight and they lock their hands and this man—*whose father is he again?*—says 1, 2, 3, and Metalhead pulls down hard. There's resistance. Oh, a bunch of strong resistance. But he ain't giving up on this. It feels good to strain his muscles, to grip this strange man's hand and push with everything he's got.

John

John isn't sure if he'd subconciously planned it all along or not, but there he was bending down and drawing a hopscotch board on the sidewalk outside of Shanna's Hardees. He'd just finished eating his cheeseburger and fries, had stepped outside and when he placed his fingers in his jacket pocket he felt a piece of sidewalk chalk. It was pink, no more than two inches long, but plenty long enough to draw what he needed.

He was on box 7 before it occurred to him this might

not be the best idea if his goal was to go unnoticed. But he was almost done and it made no sense to stop what he'd started. After sketching out the board, he wrote beside the first box, TRY IT, just like he'd seen (and done quite a few times now) on that original board at the hospital.

As he straightened up, a little girl walked and said, "Can I play?"

"Sure," John said. The girl's mother, practically a child herself, smiled at John and John blushed as he smiled back.

"Play, Mommy, come play," the girl said.

Her mother put her cell phone away and began to play. John walked back across the street to wait for his bus to deliver him back home in Greensboro.

It was after five and the sun was well on its way down and the air had turned downright cold. John watched another kid jump on the hopscotch board before disappearing into the Hardees.

He wondered if secretly he'd drawn it there for Shanna, if after work she'd see the board on her way out, and perhaps even play a game. Of course, she was no longer a child, but still, maybe she would.

When his bus pulled up, John thought of staying, of waiting to see who else might jump on the board. But it was past six and the next bus wouldn't be here for another two hours. He'd better get going.

As the bus pulled away, John looked back once more and saw a couple teenager girls, but not Shanna, start to play. They laughed and laughed and then the bus was gone onto the dark highway. When John looked back all he could see was the light from the Hardee's sign somewhere in the distance.

CEO

Ralph Davis hadn't thought about that hopscotch board again until he saw it on the local TV news. He hadn't been to the hospital in almost a week because he'd been in Seattle at a healthcare administrators' conference. But he was back in Greensboro, in his home office, working over some financial reports, when his wife, Melissa, called out for him, said something about the hospital being on the news.

Davis wondered what they could be reporting on. He didn't know of anything new going on at the hospital, and any hospital-related news was supposed to be approved by him through Janice in Public Relations. As he watched a commercial featuring a bearded man talk about the benefits of performing maintenance on your air conditioning unit throughout the year Davis grew nervous.

The news was back on and the camera panned from the hospital to the sidewalk outside the entrance, then to the hopscotch board. Davis felt his neck flash hot. He'd forgotten about the hopscotch board, but he'd told Sloan to clean it off twice already. Davis stopped listening as the reporter kept talking and kids jumped on the board behind her.

He turned the TV off and the first thing he did was call Sloan at home. "Sloan, I thought I told you to erase that damn hopscotch board."

"We did. We've done it about twenty times in the past week, but every morning it's back there again."

"Who is doing it?" Davis asked.

"I don't know."

"Get rid of it," Davis said, hanging up. He called Janice at home. "I just saw this report on the news."

"It was great, wasn't it?" she said.

"No, actually, it wasn't. You're supposed to get everything approved by me."

"I tried calling and e-mailing you, but you never responded. The hopscotch board is good news for the hospital."

"It is not good news," Davis said. "This is not a playground. What if one of those kids fall and breaks an arm and their parents sue the hospital?"

"A lot of children's hospitals have playgrounds, sir," Janice said.

"But we're not a children's hospital where they have padded floors on their playground, so when a kid falls they don't get hurt."

"Well maybe we need to add something like that here," she said. "Because I think this is about the best thing to happen to the hospital in the five years I've been here."

"I don't understand why they can't play upstairs on the pediatric floor," Davis said.

"They want to be outside."

"It's too cold."

"They're kids. The cold doesn't bother them," she said.

"I don't have time for this," he said and slammed the phone down, wondering how he got to be the head of a hospital full of idiots. He walked over to a cabinet, pulled out a bottle of whiskey and a glass, made himself a drink and swallowed a couple aspirin. He turned out the lights and told himself to concentrate on his slow, steady breathing like his therapist had told him to do when the stress headaches came. But it didn't help.

Ten minutes later, his wife opened the door and called him to dinner. His five-year-old twins, Ellie and Caroline, came running into the dining room. They hugged Davis and sat down at the table.

Ellie said, "Daddy, we saw your hospital on the news." Ellie had a tendency to talk for both of them. "Can we come and play on your hopscotch board?"

"No," he said. He couldn't remember them ever asking to come to the hospital before.

The girls looked at each other in a questioning way. "But why?" Ellie asked.

"Girls, hospitals are for making sick people better, not for playing around or games."

"But there was a girl on the news," Ellie said. "She said the hopscotch board made her feel better."

Davis could feel his headache getting worse. He needed another drink.

Melissa reached over and squeezed his hand. "Honey, it was a touching story."

"I don't understand why you girls can't just draw one in our driveway."

Ellie said, "It's not the same. You never let us do anything." She ran out of the room. Caroline shook her head at her father and followed her sister upstairs.

Melissa turned to him.

"Please don't start," he said. "Not you too."

"What's wrong with letting sick kids play a game that might make them feel better for a little while? I mean, Ralph, it's Christmas."

"What's that got to do with anything?"

"These kids are in the hospital, they don't want to be there. This gives them something to look forward to. What's the point of Christmas?"

When he didn't answer, she continued, "It's for families to be together, and by the way you better stop pushing your daughters away."

But he wasn't listening to her. He headed back to his basement office. After calling the hospital's lawyers and telling them to threaten the news station with a lawsuit, Davis logged on to his work e-mail, planning on composing an e-mail to the hospital board of directors and the staff stating that he had not approved the hopscotch board and once they found out who was drawing it that person would be reprimanded.

In the thirty minutes since the report aired, he had 54 e-mails with the word *Hopscotch* in the subject line. He tentatively started to open them—fearful of what they would say—but almost all of them were positive, praising him for what a great idea the hopscotch board was. Davis shook his head. It was the strangest damn thing.

Janice had sent an e-mail with a link to the news story. He sat back and watched the full report on his computer. It opened with shots of the hospital and the board he'd seen earlier. The reporter started talking into the camera about this mysterious board that seemed to come from nowhere.

As she spoke, patients, nurses, visitors, and even Dr. Clark, the lead pathologist, jumped on the board behind her. The camera focused on a little blonde girl wearing a yellow mask.

Davis felt something in his heart twist at the sight of this girl. She was only a couple years older than his twins. He turned his computer off and walked out the back door. He needed some fresh air, so he rolled his SUV's window down as he backed out of his driveway.

It was dark and cold when he pulled into the hospital parking deck. He headed for the entrance where the hopscotch board had been. Sloan must have had someone come and erase it as soon as they'd talked.

When he saw a couple guys from the cleaning crew

coming his way, Davis walked back to his car. It was parked on the first level so that he had a good view of the entrance.

The two men talked for a minute, but neither man bent down to re-trace the board. Ten minutes later, two nurses came outside. They were both in their 20's. One was black, one white. The two nurses pulled something from their coat pockets. At first, Davis didn't notice what it was—maybe a cell phone—but then they were both squatting down, writing something on the sidewalk. Davis knew then they were drawing a new hopscotch board.

Had they been the ones drawing it all along? He considered jumping out of his car, running up to them and getting their names, but they were taking turns hopping on the board. A couple more nurses showed up until there were five, then six and seven. He was surprised they'd come out here at night in the cold. There was something about the way they were playing, laughing the whole time even while huddled in their jackets, that Davis found touching.

He thought back to his patient care days, how sometimes he'd work a 12-hour shift and not even get a lunch. He remembered coming home, exhausted, falling asleep before Melissa finished dinner. And he remembered feeling like his bosses, and their bosses, didn't really care about him. If the hopscotch board let these nurses, and the patients, relax for a few minutes, what did it really hurt? Was it right for him to take it away?

After the nurses walked back inside, Davis leaned back in his seat. He was tired. He'd made his wife and kids mad at him. He'd yelled at Sloan and Janice, and had called his lawyer, threatening a suit. His knee jerk reaction had caused a lot of trouble.

Sitting in his car, in the hospital parking lot, Davis

knew he needed to figure out what to do next. But first he needed to rest, so he closed his eyes.

Rosa

When Rosa woke up on the morning after her report on the hopscotch board aired, she had a voice mail from her boss, Ed, telling her to get to the station as soon as she could. They needed to have a meeting. She assumed he wanted her to do a follow up story on the hopscotch board. The story had generated more e-mails and texts than any she had ever done. Part of her was surprised, but another part of her knew that people want, and need, good news in the midst of all the bad things the world throws at them on a daily basis.

On her way to the station, Rosa tried to call Janice to see if she'd received any feedback at the hospital, but Janice's phone kept going straight to voice mail.

Janice and Rosa had joked about the possibility of arranging some sort of festival for the patients and community. Prizes would be given for competing and for winning. There would be bands and balloons, maybe even face painting and Santa Claus too. They knew they were getting ahead of themselves, way ahead of themselves, but it felt good to dream.

Rosa was surprised when she walked in Ed's office and spotted Chris Laney, the TV station's attorney. Rosa had only been in one other meeting with Chris. That time it had to do with a man they'd filed a restraining order against because he was harassing her.

Before Rosa even sat down, Ed said, "We've got a

problem with the hospital hopscotch story."

His words sucked the air right out of Rosa. "What sort of problem?"

"We received a phone call from the hospital's attorney first thing this morning. He said if we mentioned the hopscotch board on the air, or our website, again they would sue."

"Can they do that?" she asked.

"Not really," Chris said. "Technically, you could stand on the sidewalk and do a report on anything, but they also threatened to take away their sponsorship. We all know how much money they give the TV station."

"But why? It doesn't make sense," Rosa said.

Chris shrugged. "Apparently, the hospital's CEO doesn't think their hospital is the right place for a child's game."

"But that's the crazy part. There's no better place," Rosa said. "So we just let it go? Let them take away the little bit of hope some of these people have?" Rosa could feel herself boiling now. "It's about these kids, Ed. This gives them something."

Ed turned to Chris who said, "What I'd suggest is we let it sit for a few days. Don't do anything and just see how it plays out. Maybe the patients can complain."

Rosa shook her head. "They have enough to worry about. They don't have time to call someone and complain."

Chris nodded. "I know what you're saying, Rosa. But trust me. Just let it sit for a few days. I bet it will blow over and the CEO and board members will come to their senses."

Rosa needed to get some fresh air, so she walked out to her car. She checked her phone and saw that Janice had tried to call twice. She'd left a message, telling Rosa to call her.

Janice answered on the third ring. "Hey, Rosa. The story looked great." Janice said.

"Thanks, but we've got some bad news," Rosa said.

"I know," Janice said. "Davis didn't like it at all. He started yelling at me, saying I didn't run the story by him, which isn't true. I tried e-mailing him multiple times, but he never responded."

"I'm sorry I dragged you into this," Rosa said. "And that he yelled at you."

"Don't worry about it," Janice said. "I just hate that he is so blind he can't see how special this hopscotch board is to the hospital and the patients. I saw the smiles on those kids' faces. We did the right thing, Rosa."

After they hung up, Rosa thought about the smiling faces of the staff and patients, and even visitors. She was thinking about the people who had called and e-mailed and texted her, telling her how much they loved the story. She knew she had to somehow continue getting the word out on this hospcotch board, but she didn't know how she could do it without the CEO's support.

She was desperate now, so she called the only person she could think of, Ray.

Ray

Ray hated to hear Rosa so upset. She had done nothing wrong. If anything, she had done everything right. She'd gone out and found a good story and reported on it. He didn't understand how the CEO could view this as a negative thing.

He didn't know much about the man. Doctors and

hospital administrators rarely have much to do with each other, but Ray needed to talk to Davis today. He told Glennis he'd be back in a half hour and to page him if anything came up.

On his way to the parking lot, he walked by the hopscotch board. There were two security guards standing where the hopscotch boards used to be. This is ridiculous, Ray thought.

"Dr. Hernandez, what are they doing?"

Ray turned. It was Emily Andrews and her parents. They looked confused. Her dad, Clay, did not look happy.

"I think there's been a misunderstanding," he said. "But I'm going to find out."

"Does this mean we can't play hopscotch anymore?" Emily asked.

"I'm going to straighten this out right now. But in the meantime you need to play inside. We can make up a board in the play room."

"But it won't be the same," she said.

"I know. Until this is straightened out, we don't have a choice."

The CEO's office was not in the hospital but in an administrative building two miles away. It was one thing to ask Rosa and the news station to not run any more stories on the boards, but to wash them away and post security guards there so the kids couldn't even play was crazy. The game got them out of their rooms and reminded them, if only for a few minutes, that they, too, were normal kids.

Emily Andrews had been in great spirits this past week, despite her chemo treatments. And it was obvious why. The hopscotch board.

Ray had not been to the CEO's office for three years,

not since his hospital orientation. All new physicians had to meet with the CEO. Ray had no clue what they had talked about on that day.

Ray walked up to the secretary outside Davis' office and said, "I'm Dr. Raymond Hernandez. I need to speak with Mr. Davis."

The secretary made a phone call and a moment later, Davis walked out of his office. "Dr. Hernandez," he said. "Come on in." He motioned toward his office.

The CEO was a short, compact man in his early fifties. His suit was expensive and grey and the skin on his face looked softer than some of Ray's pediatric patients. His eyes were puffy. He didn't look like a man who had slept well the night before.

The office was big with black leather furniture and framed photos of a pair of beautiful twin blond girls. Behind his desk was a large window overlooking the heavily-treed Latham Park bicycle trail.

"So what can I do for you, Dr. Hernandez?"

"We need to talk about the hopscotch board."

The CEO nodded. "That's right, you're married to the reporter, Rosa Hernandez. You can have your hopscotch board," he said.

Ray wondered if he heard correct. "What?"

"I overreacted."

"But I just saw two men guarding the sidewalk."

Davis shook his head. "I think our housekeeping director got tired of me calling and telling him to clean the sidewalk, so he posted a couple men from security there. I'll call them, straighten this out."

"And the lawsuit against the TV station?"

"Man, I must have got a little hot-headed last night. I'll call and apologize," Davis said. "Do you have any children, Dr. Hernandez?"

"Not yet, no," Ray said.

"When you do, don't be so busy you miss watching them grow up."

Ray didn't know what to say. The CEO had obviously had a change of heart. Maybe he'd just come to his senses. "That's good advice," Ray said.

"Tell your wife I said thanks."

"For what?" Ray asked.

"For waking me up."

When Ray didn't say anything, Davis continued, "I think I just got crazy for a while. Then my wife reminded me how these kids need something as a distraction. I kept worrying about what it would cost the hospital if one of these kids got hurt instead of how being outside playing hopscotch was helping them by making them happy for a little while."

"Sometimes we all needed to be reminded," Ray said.

"And it's Christmas and these kids are stuck here."

"You'd be giving them a great gift by letting them play," Ray said.

"It's the least I can do," Davis said. "Can I show you something?"

"Sure," Ray said. He wanted to get out of there and back to the hospital, to Rosa and his kids, but he figured the least he could do was listen to what the man said now that he'd come to his senses.

"I was looking online and found this company in Winston that makes those soft, rubber tiles you can put on the ground. That way, at least, if someone does fall they won't get hurt," Davis said. "They use them over at other hospitals."

Ray looked over at the computer screen. The company

had posted a few photos and they did show sidewalks covered with what looked like rubber tiles, an inch thick. There was even one photo of a hopscotch board made out of the tiles.

"I think it could work," Ray said.

"Good. I'm going to call them, see if they can do something like this with a section of our sidewalk there at the hospital."

"I think that's a good idea," Ray said, shaking Davis's hand.

Ray walked back out to his car. He sat there for a minute before driving back to the hospital. He wasn't quite sure what had happened to change Davis's mind. Maybe he'd just come to his senses. Maybe the Christmas spirit. Maybe pressure from people at the hospital. Whatever the reason, the kids would be happy they'd be able to play on the hopscotch board again, which would make his wife, Rosa, very happy.

Rosa

When Rosa pulled up to the hospital, Ray was squatting down, re-drawing the hopscotch board. He had called the pediatric unit and told the nurses the hopscotch board was ready for action if any of the kids wanted to come down. Rosa and Ray walked to the cafeteria for some coffee.

He told her about the security guards and going to see Davis. He said the man looked tired and admitted he'd made a big mistake. He was looking for a way to make amends.

When Ray's beeper began to buzz, he headed back

upstairs and Rosa went back outside. The sidewalk and hopscotch board were starting to fill up. There were ten people there, including Emily and Garrett and that Beth girl. Along with the kids, some of the people were employees, a few adult patients, and a couple people from the community.

Sitting at the picnic table, beside the parking garage, Rosa felt something stirring inside of her. She could not remember the last time she had been so excited about her job or her life. It was probably back when she first sat in front of a camera, back in a high school drama class. Now, she felt like she'd done something, she'd actually made a difference in people's lives.

More people continued to walk up and play on the hopscotch board. Because of the lines that were forming, a nurse drew another board, and it didn't take long before people were standing in the line for that one too.

Rosa's phone rang. It was Janice.

"You alright?" Rosa asked.

"Just got off the phone with Davis and he apologized for yelling at me, said we could do whatever we wanted with the hopscotch board," Janice said. "So let's do that festival."

"Are you serious?" Rosa asked.

"Of course."

After they hung up, Rosa watched Beth, that little girl she'd met with cerebral palsy, hop on the board. What struck Rosa about her now was how bright her red hair was. It seemed electric and alive, beautiful. She remembered Ray walking outside with Beth that day she'd filmed Emily on the sidewalk. He was holding Beth's non-contracted hand. Rosa could tell she had cerebal palsy because of the pronounced limp and the arm that was tucked in close to her body like a bird protecting a broken wing. But it was a wing they were trying to help heal.

Clay Andrews

Clay and Bev rode the elevator downstairs. Emily had just gone to sleep and Bev had said she needed to go for a walk to get some fresh air. Clay expected her to protest when he said he would go with her. They rarely left Emily alone, even when she was sleeping. But the girl had worn herself out this afternoon, playing hopscotch with her new friends, after Dr. Hernandez told them they were allowed to play outside again. Maybe Bev was just too tired to argue about it anymore.

Either way, Clay and Bev walked out into the cool night air. They walked past a couple of nurses playing on the hopscotch board and headed to the picnic table beside the parking garage. Bev pulled a cigarette out and lit it.

They had both quit smoking when they found out she was pregnant with Emily, but Bev had started up again after they received the diagnosis. Clay had not, until tonight. He took the cigarette from Bev and puffed two times; it tasted hollow and like a piece of the past. He felt the weight of his sadness and the deep start of tears, but he was so damn tired of crying and wishing for a sort of life that was not coming back.

"You all right?" she asked.

"Just peachy," he said.

"Peachy keen," they said in unison. It was something they used to say all the time when their life did seem to be pretty damn peachy keen, back before Emily got sick and they fell into this world of hospitals and treatments and what if's.

"Thank you for letting her come out here again," Clay said.

"Well, forget about the doctors, once Santa starts saying she should be allowed to go back outside, doesn't seem like I had much choice. Unless, of course, I want to officially be known as the Grinch."

"It's not like you to care what other people think," Clay said, hoping it came across as a compliment as he'd intended.

"I just got tired of fighting for the same thing, for her to lie in a bed if what she really wanted was to be outside playing."

They each took a couple puffs off the cigarette. The smoke filled the air around them. They weren't supposed to be smoking here, but it didn't matter, not to them at least. They'd been living in the here and now every day since Emily had gotten sick, so a rule like *No Smoking Allowed* didn't even register in their world.

"Tell me the truth," Bev said. "Did you send Santa in there on purpose? Did you tell him to mention the board?"

Clay raised his right hand. "Honestly, I didn't."

She nodded as if believing him. "Clay, what are we going to do?"

He didn't know if she meant right then, or the next day, or in the days and years to come. "Keep going," he said.

"But how?"

"I don't know," he said. "We'll figure it out. It's Christmas. This might be her last one. We've got to make it special."

"For her or for us?" she asked.

"Both," he said. "Whatever we do from here on out

is what we're left with. She looks good. She looks happy when she's out here."

"But pretty soon it's going to be too cold for her to come out here."

"I know, but right now it's still warm enough in the middle of the day. Maybe another week, so we've got to let her play while she can," Clay said.

"What scares me . . ." Bev started.

"What?" he asked. "Say it."

"What scares me is that she'll be in pain. It's going to be bad enough, but I'm afraid she's going to be in pain at the end. I'm afraid she's going to fall again and really get hurt and be in pain."

"They'll make her comfortable," Clay said.

"I guess. Do you think in twenty years we'll remember this hopscotch board?" She waved her arm in the general direction of the hospital, of the hopscotch board.

"I think we will. We'll remember the good stuff, not the bad."

"I don't want her to hate me," Bev said and started to cry.

Clay hugged her. "Oh, she doesn't hate you, Bev. You're her mom."

Eventually, her crying eased up. They each took a final puff of the cigarette before Clay squished it in the waist-high ashtray beside the picnic table. They held hands and walked back toward the entrance. The nurses had gone back inside, so the hopscotch board was empty now.

"Care to play a game?" he asked.

For the longest moment, she didn't say anything. She looked up toward Emily's window as if she expected the girl to be standing there, staring down at them. But the curtain was closed with only a sliver of light peaking through. She tried to push aside her thought that soon when she looked up, or around the corner, Emily would not be there.

"A quick one," she said.

They played the game in silence, and Clay was surprised at how athletic Bev was. He'd forgotten she'd played softball in college and used to run three miles a day back when they started dating. All he'd seen her do in what felt like forever was sit in a chair, holding their daughter's hand.

After she squatted down and re-traced the hopscotch board, Clay hugged her and for the first time in months she didn't push him away. She hugged him back, her hot breath on his ear, their hearts thumping together.

Metalhead Mike

Metalhead has the covers pulled up to his waist. He's listening to his uncle tell a story about playing football back in high school. He was a wide receiver. His uncle is tall and has a beard and while he is not his father's brother, Metalhead remembers the two men sneaking off to go outside and smoke. He remembers watching them through the kitchen window, how Uncle Bobby would talk and his father would nod. How Uncle Bobby could always get him laughing.

"So you have to grip the ball correctly to throw a spiral," Uncle Bobby says. He holds the ball out to Metalhead, who takes it in his hand, wraps his fingers around the white string there, the laces. Uncle Bobby puts his hand on top of Metalhead's as if to push it down on top of the ball, as if to show him how much to squeeze.

"Was my dad any good at football?" Metalhead asks.

"No," Uncle Bobby says. "He loved to watch it, but he wasn't what you'd call athletically-gifted."

"Was I?"

Uncle Bobby looks past Metalhead and tries to smile in the general direction of the wall and the web of oxygen tubing up there. "Maybe when you get out, we can practice all summer and sign you up for a team."

"Maybe," Metalhead says.

"I gotta run, Mike. You get some rest." Uncle Bobby leans forward and pats Metalhead's knee twice, then turns to leave.

Beneath the sheets, Metalhead squeezes the football as tight as he can. He doesn't want to hear anything else about how his father is not athletically-gifted, doesn't want to think about Santa Claus or about the Physical Therapy that busts his butt everyday. And he doesn't want to remember anything—not now, not today. All he wants is to drift off and take what sleep offers, a chance to close his eyes and wake up, hours later, only to realize all of this has been a dream.

But as he starts to drift off, he sees himself in Mrs. Stewart's 4th grade class, taking a spelling test. The words—*homework* and *homeschool*—don't seem that hard, but he's tired of looking at his paper, waiting for Mrs. Stewart to call out the next word, so he looks over at a girl named Paige and she smiles at him. She's a little chunky girl with brown hair. She's wearing a yellow dress. They've been in class together since kindergarten.

It's just a smile, but enough to surprise him and for a moment he can't hear what Mrs. Stewart says, what word she has announced but he knows she said something because the rest of the kids have lowered their heads and started writing on their lined, white paper.

He turns back to Paige, but she's no longer looking at him, and he wonders if he imagined the whole thing. If she never looked at him at all. If she had only looked up searching for the correct spelling of that word, as if it might be floating somewhere in the classroom air.

He turns to Mrs. Stewart and she is mouthing another word but he doesn't hear what it is. He could raise his hand and ask her to repeat the word, but he knows she's said it three times already. She always says the word three times.

Metalhead is mad at himself for looking over at Paige, for letting himself be distracted because spelling is a subject he is good at, or at least used to be good at, and if he earns an A on a spelling test he gets something cool at home, like an extra 15 minutes of screen time everyday for a week. But now it looks like he might have messed up his perfect record of all A's because he hasn't even written down the last two words Mrs. Stewart has said.

When he looks at Paige again, she is not looking at him. She is chewing the eraser on her pencil and staring at the paper in front of her.

Later, after the test, they are at recess, on the playground and Paige is playing hopscotch with a girl named Cara. What he wants more than anything at that moment is for Paige to ask him if he wants to play with them, but she doesn't. He'd like to walk over there and ask if he can play, but he's not that good at hopscotch, so he watches them from a distance for a few minutes until Mrs Stewart blows the whistle, indicating recess is over.

That night, after his mother leaves for her usual after-dinner walk, Metalhead sits on the couch next to his father who is watching a Braves game. He can't remember who they're playing, but he knows it's the Braves because that is the only baseball team his father cares about. For Father's Day last year, the whole family drove five hours to Atlanta to watch the Braves play the Dodgers.

Metalhead asks his father if he can help him get better at hopscotch and his father says sure though there's something in his father's *sure* that gives Metalhead some serious doubts. His father pulls his small black cell phone from his shorts pocket, types something, and then the two of them sit on the couch and watch a video of some kids— girls, of course—playing hopscotch. After a minute or two, his father says, "I think we can figure this out. Let's go give it a try."

Out on the driveway, they realize they don't have any chalk, just a long stretch of pavement. But they do have a lot of small white stones bordering the walkway leading to the front door. From this his father creates an uneven board in the following shape: 1 box, 2 boxes, 1 box, 2 boxes, 1 box, 2 boxes, 1 box. He looks at Metalhead and says, "Ten, right?"

Metalhead agrees, remembering the board at school, and they start practicing, hopping from single box to double box to single. Metalhead's father is even less coordinated than he is. Still, he tries, and he stands there and cheers Metalhead on when Metalhead knows he'd rather be inside watching the Braves game, watching Chipper Jones play his final season.

His father tries again and only gets to the seventh box before losing his balance and falling into the grass. They hear clapping and look up to see his mother, laughing, walking toward them. She has snuck up on them. "What in the world?" she asks.

Metalhead is sweating. His father is sweating too.

"You two are about as coordinated as a pair of three-legged lizards," his mother says.

Metalhead has no idea what that means, but she holds his hand and hops with him all the way to the end of the board and back again. He knows if he were to try this again at school tomorrow it still wouldn't be pretty. His mother, though, seems like a pro at this game. It's as if women and girls have secret abilities, things he will never understand. His father is still sitting on the grass, smoking a cigarette and watching the two of them. And when Metalhead smiles, his father smiles back, wiping the sweat from his forehead.

CEO

Davis looked up at the clock. It was only 2:30, but he couldn't stay in this office any longer. Not today. Things had gotten interesting since they'd run that news report. It turned out most members of the hospital board were fine with the hopscotch board, but a few of the older, stodgier ones were not. Still, he'd done his best to convince them not to worry. He told them he had it under control.

He'd spent the morning over at Baptist Hospital with a sales rep from the company that makes those soft tiles. It was true they did feel pretty soft and he'd even fallen to his knees at one point to see what it would feel like, and it wasn't hard at all. Of course, when he fell on purpose, a pair of kids playing outside laughed. A grown man in a suit falling down in the middle of their playground. Who wouldn't laugh at that?

So he was definitely going to buy the tiles, but first they

had to decide if they wanted a full playground or only an area for the hopscotch boards. He was fine either way. He'd let the pediatric department decide.

In the meantime, he'd told Janice she could go ahead and publicize the hopscotch board any way she wanted. When she mentioned a festival, he said that sounded like a great idea. If it made people happy, he said, go ahead. He didn't think he'd be able to get the tiles installed in the next couple weeks, before the full cold of winter kicked in, but still he didn't want to stop anything that was going to happen with the hopscotch board.

He couldn't remember the last time he had left work early, but he wanted to see his girls. Maybe he would surprise them. Show up at the house and take them to a movie or over to the country club for a swim in the indoor pool. Whatever they wanted.

On the drive home, he decided to swing by the hospital. He would not go inside, but he wanted to see how many people would actually be outside playing on the board on a Thursday afternoon. Janice had told him it was normal for ten or twenty people to be there at a time.

Davis parked in the doctors' lot and walked around the corner, toward the front entrance. There were a good twenty people out there. The one board had turned into four. He blinked and looked again. His wife and daughters were there, on the sidewalk, playing. His first thought was confusion, followed by sadness that he himself hadn't brought them here.

He heard the familiar sound of his daughters' laughter and he felt something in his chest lift. When his wife, Melissa, looked up, she smiled and waved and Davis did the same back to her, and his girls were running toward him, laughing, saying "Daddy, Daddy, come play with us."

He couldn't remember the last time they had asked him that. They used to when they were smaller, but he was always so busy, working sixty to seventy hours a week. He'd told them *no* so many times they'd stopped asking him to play.

Now, each girl held one of his hands.

"You'll have to show me how," he said. He had forgotten the most basic rules of this simple childhood game. And so they took him by the hand, both talking a million miles an hour with their voices light and happy, and after he got the rules down they played and played and played until they were all tired.

Afterwards, they drove home and ate spaghetti and meatballs for dinner. For the longest time, he had felt distanced from his girls, felt as he'd somehow lost his connection with them, but now he'd found it again. At least, he had started. Through a hopscotch board drawn by someone, or a group of someones, at his hospital.

Garrett

It was time for Garrett to go home. His numbers were looking better and he wouldn't need another treatment for at least two weeks. The doctors said they could do the treatment as an outpatient.

While he was looking forward to going home, he knew he'd miss his new friends—Metalhead Mike and Beth and Emily. But his mother said that when they got out of the hospital, they could all come to his house. They could even do a sleepover, and there was no reason to believe they wouldn't still be friends.

As Garrett's mom got his discharge paperwork together, he and Emily snuck away to the playroom. They sat together on the oversized red bean bag.

"You can come to my house," Garrett said.

"I might not get to leave the hospital again," she said.

"Can I come see you here?"

"Of course you can, Garrett-Carrot." She had started calling him that and while it was silly, he didn't mind.

He told her they could do a sleepover here at the hospital. Maybe he could put a cot in her room or something. Emily said that sounded good to her, but right now she was so tired from playing. He scooted over to her beanbag, and they rested their heads on each other's shoulders.

She wanted to ask him to kiss her because she didn't think she'd ever get another chance. But she didn't know how to ask him to do something she'd never done before.

It was only after she'd given up trying to figure out how to ask that he turned toward her and kissed her forehead. Blushing, she lifted her mask and he kissed her on the lips. It wasn't a long, passionate movie kiss, but a simple peck, lip to lip. Still, it was a kiss.

She giggled and he did too. They leaned into each other's shoulder and closed their eyes, trying to hold onto this for as long as they could.

Beth

Beth held her hand out, so Emily could paint her fingernails. The polish was pink with tiny silver specks and Emily kept saying, "Hold still, hold still," but Beth couldn't stop laughing. She'd never had another girl paint her fingernails like this for her. Her mother was usually the one who did it.

Emily said, "I love this color."

Beth did too. Emily's mother had set a small bottle of the polish under Emily's Christmas tree that morning. Beth had been bored with the TV program her mother was watching, so she'd walked over to Emily's room and found her painting her nails. Emily's mother had stepped out of the room to make a phone call.

"You nervous about your surgery?" Emily asked.

"A little," Beth said. "I guess. I mean if it will work. If I'll be able to make necklaces and stuff with my fingers then it'll be worth it."

Over the past couple days, she and Emily had watched TV together, and Emily read books and played hopscotch with her. Beth had not had a friend like Emily in a long time. Back in pre-school and into kindergarten, she had friends, but with each school year the difference between herself and the other kids grew greater, so much so that she was no longer like them. She was different, the girl who walked funny and kept her arms against her side.

But Emily talked to her about boys and cute Garrett and his crazy-pretty mom. They talked about songs they liked and TV shows and vanilla ice cream and cats. They talked about the sounds of the hospital, the night beeps and jagged lines on the monitors. They looked in each other's eyes and laughed and talked.

Even though Beth wasn't as good at hopscotch as Emily, she loved playing the game with her because Emily never made fun of her like the kids in school. So whether it was on the hopscotch board or in one of their hospital rooms, they were in this together. Friends.

"Do you ever get scared here in the hospital?" Beth

asked.

"Sure," Emily said, looking up. "Don't you?"

"Yeah, but I like the nurses. They're really nice."

"Are you afraid of the pain from the surgery?" Emily asked.

"It usually doesn't hurt too bad. They give you a lot of medicine."

Emily nodded. "My elbow still hurts from when I fell, and the needles hurt."

"I don't mind the needles. Not anymore. It's like homework, something you have to do even when you don't want to. Do you think you can come to my birthday party in March?" Beth asked.

"Of course," Emily said, holding onto Beth's contracted arm and trying to get the polish on.

The door opened and Emily's evening nurse, Stephanie, walked in the door. She was a tall, black woman. "About time for bed you two."

"We're almost done," Beth said.

"Five minutes. You've got a big day tomorrow with the hopscotch festival. I've got a feeling one of you will win it all." Stephanie opened the door to leave and turned back to the girls. "Now you've only got four minutes."

When the door shut behind the nurse, Beth said, "Five minutes, girls," and the two of them started laughing.

"Hold on. I'm almost done," Emily said.

"Tomorrow is going to be so amazing," Beth said.

"You got that right. Stick with me, Bethy-Beth, we're going to have a blast."

Beth leaned into her friend and thought she was already having a blast. It was hard for her to imagine it could get much better than this.

John

John leaned forward, looking through the jewelry store display case. He wanted a simple gold necklace, nothing too fancy, something Shanna could wear all the time.

"Can I help you?" The salesman was tall and wearing a dark suit. He stood behind the counter.

"Can I see this one?" John asked, pointing at the gold chain with the small gold cross.

The salesman smiled at him. John was sure if the man knew he'd been in prison he would not have smiled. He handed John the necklace. "For your wife?"

"What?" John's face flushed.

The man nodded toward John's gold wedding ring, which he still wore. In fact, he'd never seriously considered taking it off.

"No," John said, relaxing. "My daughter. She's seventeen."

"Oh, well this will be perfect then."

The necklace felt light in his hand. It cost $250.

John nodded. "Yes, I'll take it."

As the man wrapped it for him, John looked around the jewelry store at the customers finishing their Christmas shopping and he couldn't help but smile. It felt good to be part of a world that didn't live in his grief, a world where happiness was right around the corner, even if only temporary.

Back outside the store, it was getting dark. He squeezed the jewelry box in his jacket pocket. In the last three months, he'd also bought Shanna a silver necklace, a couple bracelets, a ring and two pairs of earrings. Each one seemed like the right gift at the time, a gift for a reunion he hoped was in the near future, but which he knew might not happen at all.

Still, these gifts offered him a little hope, the thought, no matter how unlikely, that he'd actually get to give them to her this Christmas.

After walking around the shopping center, John stopped at Jason's Deli for a bowl of chicken noodle soup. As the soup warmed him, he looked out across the parking lot at the row of crepe myrtles wrapped in bright red and green and blue Christmas lights. And this made him smile. He needed to stop on the way home tomorrow and get a few lights for the inside of his apartment, maybe a thin strand to go around one of the windows or the balcony.

He took a deep breath and blew it out and remembered one Christmas—he couldn't be sure but thought Shanna was four that year—and she'd helped him with the family Christmas lights. They'd strung them across the living room floor, making sure they all lit properly. Her job was to find the ones that didn't work.

When she found one, she would call him over. He'd replace the small bulb and when it lit up, she would clap with excitement. While she wanted to go outside to help him hang the lights, he said she couldn't because it was too cold. After he and Tara hung them, they bundled Shanna in her big purple jacket and brought her outside to see the house all lit up. John remembered taking a picture of her standing on the lawn, as the sun went down, and the lights shined behind her. She had her hands and purple gloves out by her side as if to say, look what we've done. That picture had been on their mantelplace on the day of the accident. He remembered looking at it briefly before they went to that party at his professor's house. He didn't know what had happened to the picture, but he could see his little girl, with her arms stretched out to her side, as if he were holding the picture in his hand right now.

"Are you done, sir?"

John looked up. It was one of the Deli workers, holding his hand out for John's food tray. He'd finished his soup without even realizing it. He held the tray up to the young man. "Thank you," John said. John looked at his watch. He had fifteen minutes to get to the bus stop for the 9:20 bus.

He stopped at a shoe store and looked through the window, but the store was empty. The salespeople already gone for the day. He felt the chalk in his pocket and knew. John squatted down and started to draw another hopscotch board. He couldn't really say why he drew the boards other than the hope they might give someone else a bit of happiness.

"What's that?"

John stood and saw the homeless man in a dirty brown jacket and old ragged beard. "Drawing a little hopscotch board for the kids," John said.

The man walked toward the board and stopped shy of the # 1 box. "Hopscotch, huh? I used to play this with my kids," he said. He took a quick breath, sending a stream of steam through the air before he hopped through the board without any problem whatsoever.

John was surprised. The man was large and didn't look the least bit athletic.

"Thanks," the man said. "I guess Christmas has come early this year."

John didn't quite know what to say, and in the brief silence, the man turned and walked away. John watched him go. Tomorrow, he knew, someone else would jump here and be happy. Someone might jump on the other ten or so boards he'd drawn around town and be happy. This was more than he expected, back when he was in prison, but still he needed to reach Shanna somehow. Tomorrow, at the festival, would be about as good a chance as he would get.

Rosa

On the night before the hopscotch festival, Rosa couldn't sleep. She was excited and nervous. This was important and she wanted everything to be perfect. She had continued to stop by the hospital every day to watch the flow of people who came to play hopscotch. The single board she had seen that first time had grown into four. This, she knew, had touched a nerve with many people.

She also couldn't sleep because she wanted to talk to Ray. While he was in the shower, washing off another long day at the hospital, she thought once again about the festival and wondered if she and Janice had gotten everything ready. Janice had done the bulk of the work, setting up vendors while Rosa concentrated on getting the word out by doing another report on the hopscotch board, announcing the festival. She replied to every e-mail that came her way. She'd answered questions about the festival for a half-dozen news station in North Carolina, and even did a phone interview with a reporter from CNN.

Ray walked into the bedroom and climbed under the sheets.

"How was work?" she asked.

"Good. The kids are all excited about the festival tomorrow."

Rosa smiled. "I'm almost ready," she said

"I think everyone at work is ready too," he said.

"No," she said. "I mean about starting a family."

"Really?"

"By next summer," she said. "I promise."

He laughed. Then he kissed her. And she kissed him, and Ray leaned over and turned out the light.

Metalhead Mike

Metalhead climbs under the covers and closes his eyes to see what will come. They're running late. His mother is upstairs still getting ready and his father is watching a football game. It's early November and although his father mowed the yard earlier in the day there are already red and yellow and orange leaves covering the ground.

Metalhead turns away from the backyard and gets himself some apple juice. He doesn't want to go to his aunt and uncle's on this Sunday afternoon. He wants to sit in his room, in his big comfortable brown chair and play his video games. Or he wants to lie on the floor and see how many times he can throw the tennis ball up in the air and catch it without it hitting the floor. His record is 78 times.

But it's his aunt and uncle's twenty-fifth anniversary, so according to his mother, they have to go though no one seems in any rush. He sits on the couch, beside his father, who says, "You ready, kiddo?"

"Waiting on you," Metalhead says with a smile, not looking up from the videogame in his hands. Metalhead thinks his dad looks tired, like maybe he's gained weight.

His beard is starting to have little patches of grey and white stubble. Metalhead thinks his father is getting old.

"Do we really have to go?" Metalhead asks.

His dad smiles. "If it was up to me we'd sit here in front of the TV and watch football, make some chili, and call it a day."

"So why don't we do that?"

"Because it's your mother's sister's anniversary."

They hear a door slam upstairs and his dad clicks the TV off and stands up and nods to Metalhead to head over to the door. When his mom makes it around the corner, she says, "I'm sorry. I didn't know you were waiting for me."

"Whenever you're ready, love," his dad says and winks at Metalhead. Metalhead shakes his head and laughs as they head out the door.

His aunt lives about twenty minutes away. Metalhead figures he's been on this road a thousand times before. He knows where the Circle K is and the BP where his dad stops sometimes to buy beer or cigarettes or gas. He knows they pass a Harris Teeter where you can get free sugar cookies. He knows all this but today he doesn't look up. He is playing his videogame, bent over in the back seat, his thumbs working their magic.

His parents are talking about his Auntie Michelle. His mom is saying to not mention her job. There's been some changes at the office and she doesn't want to talk about it. And while he usually listens to their conversations and plays his videogames at the same time, today he doesn't want to hear about his aunt and her job, so he leans down and focuses on the videogame, on Mario and Princess Peach. His parent's voices are still there, but only a slight buzz. In another five or ten seconds, he will hear his mother scream, feel the impact, the crush of the car, feel everything change. But for now, he is in his game, and it still seems possible he might be able to save this videogame princess with his own bare hands.

CEO

The morning of the festival, Davis received a phone call from Jim Boylston. Boylston was on the hospital's board of trustees. He was a rich old man who'd made his money in dry cleaning. Davis had always respected him because of his success and work habits. He still worked seven days a week though he hadn't needed to in decades.

Davis believed he, too, had worked hard to get where he was. He was not a doctor's kid who went to all the best schools and been handed a hospital administrative job. No, he'd completed his Physical Therapy degree while working as a transporter in the Radiology department.

Three years into his job as a Physical Therapist he became a supervisor and continued to put in the long hours and moved up to his department's director within ten years. Davis went back to school to get his MBA, and kept working his way up the administration ladder until he earned the CEO job five years ago.

"How are you, Jim?" Davis asked.

"Not so good, I'm afraid," Boylston said.

Davis's first thought was he might be sick. The man was in his early seventies. "What's going on?"

"Watching the news this morning I saw they were going ahead with that hopscotch festival thing."

"Yes, sir." It was clear to Davis now why he was calling. Boylston had been one of the few members of the board who had not been happy when the first report on the hopscotch board aired.

"I'm a little surprised. I thought you had taken care of all this," Boylston said.

"I did, sir."

"Well, I just got off the phone with Luke and Grant and Walter and we have some serious reservations about this whole thing." Luke and Grant and Walter were three of the hospitals' oldest and wealthiest board members.

"Let me explain, sir," Davis said. "When I first noticed the board, I made the cleaning crew wash it away, but someone, and nobody knows who, drew a new one each time it was erased. The hospital staff and patients started using it, playing on it. People from the community stop by to play. Even my girls have played on it."

"That's very touching, Ralph. The point is we don't want our hospital turned into a circus. If you want to keep your job, you'd better call this off. Do you understand me?"

Davis knew the man's face was probably bright red by now. He'd seen him in enough board meetings to know how he got when he was mad, or passionate, about an issue. Davis took a couple quick breaths. He thought of his house, his cars, the sprawling yard and two vacation houses—one at the beach and one at the mountains. And he thought about his daughters, his wife, his family, and what the hopscotch board had done for them and the people who worked at the hospital, and the patients.

It was the first time in a while that he felt like he was actually helping someone instead of trying to make money for the hospital. And it was the first time in a long time that he felt a connection with his family.

"Loud and clear," Davis said.

"Good," Boylston said. "So you'll call this thing off?"

"Not a chance, sir."

Davis hung the phone up and smiled at the Santa outfit hung over his sofa.

Emily

From her window, Emily could see people starting to gather on the sidewalk. She wished she could run down there, but she had to wait. Her mother was out talking to one of the nurses, and her father wasn't back yet. He'd gone home to bring her mother some more clothes.

When the door opened, Emily stepped away from the window. Her mother was holding a cup of coffee. Her hair was still a little messy from where she'd slept in the chair. One of her parents slept here almost every night. At first this was because of her condition, but now she'd given them something else to worry about with her attempted escape.

"Sleep okay?" her mother asked.

"Pretty good."

"You've got a big day ahead of you here."

"I know," Emily said.

She climbed back onto her bed while her mother sat in the big brown chair. "Thanks, Mom," Emily said.

"For what?"

"For letting me go play outside again."

Her mother sipped her coffee slowly, as if taking her

time, trying to decide what to say next. "When I was a girl, your Grandma Rosie would take me to the library every Sunday and let me choose five books. Sometimes this would take five minutes, sometimes an hour. I'd read the books that week, and be ready for another trip to the library the following Sunday."

Emily wasn't sure why her mother was telling her this story. She rarely talked about her mother who used to own a half dozen laundromats in Georgia, back before she died when Emily was only two.

"So we'd go every Sunday from the time I was five until I was fifteen. At fifteen, she thought I was old enough to go on my own and I suppose I was if I actually went there, but I didn't. I went to see your father. We'd meet at the movies or the drug store or the park and we'd ride around. Of course, I loved being with your father, but I wished she'd continued to go with me to the library. I wish I would have done what she'd asked me to.

"What I remember was the drive there. We'd leave your grandfather back at the house, so he could watch football or something and we'd drive to the library. Sunday afternoons were the best time. It was quiet out and a lot of people stayed home. We'd walk into the library and Grandma would lift her arms to me as if to say here, choose something, there's a whole world, just choose what you want. And she'd meet me at the checkout counter, look over what I'd picked and nod whether she approved or not.

"Back at the house, I'd pick one of my books and curl up on my bed and read the afternoon away."

Emily still wasn't sure she understood the point of her mother's story, so she said, "It sounds fun, the library, but why are you telling me this?"

Her mother sat on the edge of the bed and patted Emily's leg. "I guess I always meant to take you to the library," she said. "But I didn't. Each year I told myself we'd start the tradition on your next birthday."

"It's okay, Mom. I don't like to read as much as you do."

Her mother laughed as she reached over and hugged Emily. "You ready to have fun today?"

"It's gonna be awesome," Emily said. "The most awesomest awesome."

Her mother said, "Yes, the most awesomest awesome, that's you."

Dr. Boles

Dr. Boles stopped by the hospital on the way to his 11 o'clock tee time. He was playing a threesome with two other surgeons. They played together every Saturday unless one of them was on call.

Dr. Boles was surprised when he pulled into the doctor's parking lot. There were only a few cars; but there were a lot of people. It looked more like a circus, or some sort of county fair, than a hospital. He passed a small train that drove kids around the parking lot. He passed two of those tall bouncy things with kids in line ready to bounce.

After rounding on his patients, Dr. Boles headed back out, knowing he had to get going to make his tee time. He'd asked one of the nurses what was going on outside and she'd told him it was a hopscotch festival.

Outside again, Dr. Boles looked around the festival. There were a good number of patients here, but he also spotted Dylan Mathew, a GI doctor. There were nurses and X-ray techs he recognized. He spotted Beth Hardin, that little girl he was scheduled to do surgery on Monday morning.

Beth waved at him and he waved back. A little boy walked up to him with a bag of blue and red cotton candy. He held the bag up to Dr. Boles.

"What can I do for you?" Dr. Boles asked.

The little boy stared at him and said, "Open."

Dr. Boles realized a twisty tie kept the bag closed, so he untied this and handed it back to the boy who ran off toward one of the hopscotch boards. And for some reason he couldn't quite explain, perhaps to make sure he found his parents, Dr. Boles followed the boy back into the crowd.

On the board, a couple of teenagers were running through the game pretty quickly. And he couldn't help but think of Myles again as he had that first day he saw the hopscotch board on his way into the hospital. He was embarrassed to admit he couldn't remember ever seeing him play this game. He tried hard to search his memory for a scene of Myles hopping and laughing, but no such memory came to mind.

Dr. Boles pulled his cell phone out, found his son's number under Contacts and pushed Talk. While Myles called home every weekend, he hadn't spoken to his father in almost a month. He always seemed to call when Dr. Boles was out playing golf or dictating old charts at the office. And when they did talk it always turned to work and some interesting case or patient Myles had encountered and wanted to tell his father about. Dr. Boles hung up when the call went to voice mail.

When he looked up again, he noticed that Beth girl was waving him over. He watched her jump, the way her one leg stayed back just a little. He clapped as she ran up to him. "Imagine what I'll be able to do after the surgery," she said.

He resisted the urge to fall into doctor speak, about how not all results from surgery were as great as we hoped for. Instead, he said, "It's going to be great. You're going to be able to do anything you want."

"Thank you, Dr Boles," she said and hugged him before running back to the other children.

He'd fixed so many bones over the years, everything from the skateboarder who falls and breaks a wrist to the MVA trauma patient with the compound fracture, and the elderly with their old and ruined hips and knees, but what he was doing for Beth was different. It was, he realized now, offering hope. She would not be cured, would not be able to do everything, but she would have so many more options than she did now.

When his phone buzzed in his pocket, he pulled it out, thinking it might be Myles. It was a text from one of his golfing buddies asking where he was and if he was still coming to play. He typed back, *Go ahead without me.*

He walked toward the hopscotch boards, toward the patients, not sure what he was going to do. Perhaps he'd offer help and support if some fell. Perhaps he'd just stand by and clap as they played their game. Either way, he'd watch them play and he might even join them too.

John

The morning of the hopscotch festival John walked to the hospital. It was a beautiful, December day—Carolina blue sky and sunshine, one of the last ones they would get before the cold of winter really settled in. John had called his sister-in-law three times over the last couple days and asked her to bring Shanna. At first Angelina said she wasn't sure if that was such a good idea. But by the third time, she'd said she would at least try. She said the girl was confused, and even a little scared, about meeting her father. John could understand that.

But he also knew if he had a chance to see his daughter, this would be the day. That's why he had shaved his beard and got a haircut yesterday and why he'd gone out and bought a nice, crisp new shirt and slacks at Sears. That's why he had the brand new gold cross necklace gold in his pocket.

As he rounded the corner on Elm Street, he noticed the row of cars and the news vans along with the crowd of people walking across the street. It didn't look like the same hospital. He wondered for the hundredth time who had drawn that first hopscotch board and started all this. He wondered if that person had any idea what the result would be. John didn't think there was any way they could have.

John had washed the hopscotch board away a half-dozen times when his boss asked him to, but each time when he returned later to re-draw it, someone had already re-drawn the board. Sometimes it was even re-drawn within an hour.

He'd considered hiding somewhere after he'd washed it off just to see if he could spot whoever it was that was doing this. But he decided against it. Life, he knew, was short on mysteries, and this was one he didn't mind leaving unsolved.

He walked around, listened to the kids laughing, the

sound of an announcer saying a new game would begin in a few minutes. He sat on a bench twenty or so feet from the boards and looked around. He could see that pretty newscaster lady talking to some kids. And he could see his boss, Sloan, and his three little girls.

But among these people having fun, John still felt like an outsider, as if this was a life he didn't deserve. He'd made a mistake. He'd been in an accident. He'd had three beers at a party. He'd swerved to avoid hitting a possum, and his wife had died.

John felt the buzzing in his front pocket. It was his cell phone. When John pulled it out, he saw Angelina's name and number. He almost didn't answer it, not wanting to hear his sister-in-law explain why she couldn't bring his daughter to him. But he did answer.

"Hello," he said.

For a moment there was no response, only the heavy emptiness of a silent phone in his hand.

"Angelina?"

"Daddy." Her voice sent shocks through the phone line. He couldn't breathe as the goosebumps raised on his arms.

"Shanna," he said. "Is that you?"

"Yeah," she said. "How are you?"

He laughed. "Happy, thrilled, every good word you can think of."

"I want to see you," she said. "Aunt Angelina told me about the phone calls you made, about how you asked about me and all the letters you sent that I never got."

And John held the phone against his ear, tried not to burst out crying. "Yes, baby," he said.

"Maybe we can go out to dinner or something," she said.

"Yes, I'd like that," he said.

"Me too."

John leaned back against the bench and told himself to breathe. His baby girl was on the phone talking to him.

CEO

Davis climbed out of his SUV, dressed as Santa, with his two girls dressed in green elf costumes. He'd jumped at the idea when Melissa first suggested it the day before.

They had barely made it around the corner when a young boy yelled, "It's Santa," and started running toward him.

Davis had hoped to play a game of hopscotch with his girls, but it was pretty clear that wasn't going to happen right away. The kids started to crowd around him: 5, 10, as many 15. He walked over to the bench and his elf daughters each sat on one side of him.

Again, Davis was surprised at the number of people from the community who came to see, and play on, the hopscotch boards. The first kid in line to see him was a skinny little boy, no older than three or four. He hopped up on Davis' leg and stared into his eyes as if to say, "Are you really Santa?"

"Well, Merry, Merry Christmas, young man. What would you like for Christmas?"

"My daddy to get out of the hospital," the boy said and smiled.

"Yes, that would be good," Davis said. "Would you like any other gifts?"

"A baseball, so my dad and me can play catch again."

Davis tried to smile through the fuzzy, white beard. "Alright, we'll see what we can do about getting you a new baseball." Davis looked up at the boy's mother and they shared a smile.

"Thank you, Santa," the boy said, then climbed off Davis' lap, grabbed his mother's hand, and ran back into the crowd. Ellie and Caroline were handing out candy canes to the other children in line.

Another kid, this time a girl, hopped up on his lap, Davis looked over and saw his wife, standing about twenty or so yards away, beyond the rows of hopscotch boards. She lifted a hand to her lips as if to stop herself from crying or smiling. He couldn't really tell which. But still he waved to her and she waved back and he could feel the warmth of his daughters on either side of him and Davis felt something in his chest that he knew must be love, a thing he'd forgotten about for a while, but something he'd been lucky enough to remember, to find and hold again.

Metalhead Mike

Even though they are having a festival, which means free games and food, Metalhead Mike still doesn't get the point of all this hopscotch stuff, but he's decided his Uncle Bobby is pretty cool. The two of them are playing catch with a football.

Metalhead Mike's plan is to keep lifting weights, to keep getting stronger until he can throw this football across the whole parking lot like his uncle. Metalhead wonders if he and his father used to play catch. He doesn't remember, but he does remember his father's name was Joe. He wore suits and worked in an office. Metalhead remembers his cologne too, sweet yet manly, mixed with a cigarette smell. It was his father's smell.

Metalhead is pretty sure he remembers what happened to his parents, the wreck on his way to his aunt and uncle's anniversary party. A part of him would like to hold out hope his parents are on another floor of the hospital, maybe up in ICU. Perhaps they're both in comas and will wake up this afternoon and come looking for him, but Metalhead knows that's not going to happen. It's not that he doesn't believe in miracles, but there's a hollow feeling inside of him that tells him they are gone, that he's all alone here in this hospital. But maybe he's not all alone because Uncle Bobby is yelling, "Stay with me, Mike. Pay attention."

His uncle throws the football. The ball is a spiraled bullet coming at his chest, but Metalhead's knees go all wonky. He has to catch the ball. Everything in the whole wide world depends on him catching this pass. He steadies himself, extends his arms, then bam the ball hits him in the chest, takes his breath for a moment.

I caught it, Metalhead says, *I caught it*. He lifts the ball above his head, and Uncle Bobby is running toward him with his hand in the air and they high five there in the soft grass beside the parking lot. Two hands slapping, stinging. It feels good to Metalhead Mike. So good.

Stan

Stan wheeled himself up the sidewalk. He'd seen a

report on the evening news about the hopscotch festival and asked Jay if he wanted to go. Since leaving the hospital, Stan had decided he would do one of those wheelchair races and he'd taken a part time job with Jay at his insurance agency. It might not be the most exciting job, but it got him out of the house and might lead to a career, a way to make a living and be independent again.

Stan spotted Rosa, that TV reporter, talking to a man in a suit. He considered going up to her, telling her how playing hopscotch had inspired him, but decided not to. It seemed enough that he was here now with his brother.

"You ready?"

Stan turned. A nurse handed him a piece of sidewalk chalk and motioned toward an empty hopscotch board. He heard the helicopter overhead and remembered the blue sky as the medics pulled him out of that desert. He remembered that medic Jo-Jo was wearing a yellow pin on his helmet with the band Nirvana's logo. He remembered thinking, *Man, I could use some Nirvana.*

"Toss it," Jay said, pulling Stan back to the here and now, to the hopscotch board and the kids laughing around him. To the pretty reporter in her blue dress. To Santa Claus and a couple elves walking through the crowd, waving.

Someone was coughing and when he looked up he saw that blond girl he'd seen on the board the day he'd left the hospital. She pushed her IV pole and took her place in line. Stan could tell she was smiling through the yellow mask she wore. She would get her chance to jump. She would at least be given that much. Stan closed his eyes, said a prayer for this tiny angel, and threw the stone to start another game of his own.

Emily

When Emily walks outside for the hopscotch festival, a parent on each side of her, she is surprised to see so many people here. There are TV reporters and cameras and patients and doctors and nurses and clowns and Beth and over there is Metalhead Mike. Of course, Metalhead Mike isn't playing the game. Instead, he's off to the side with his arms folded across his chest like he's mad at the world, squeezing a football.

Santa Claus and a couple elves are hopping on one of the boards. Some smaller kids are chasing Santa, trying to get him to hug them and eventually he stops hopping and sits on the bench, a kid on each leg, taking last-minute orders for Christmas, which is less than a week away now. She wonders if he's the same Santa that visited her in her room, that convinced her mother to finally let her go back outside on the hopscotch board again.

Garrett is talking to Dr. S who is trying to give him a green lollipop. Garrett looks good and strong in his blue and white striped jacket, even stronger than he'd looked when he left the hospital. Emily thinks he looks like a million bucks.

Garrett looks up and spots Emily. Before she can even wave, he runs toward her and gives her a big hug. He kisses her again on the forehead, as she hugs him back, squeezing as tight as she can. Over his shoulder, Emily smiles at Dr. S. The woman waves to her and lifts her hands in the air as if to say today is your day, Suzy Q.

Beth and Holly—yes Holly Everhart!!—walk up to them. Holly and Emily hug and lock arms and start to spin around, like they used to do in their own back yards. Over by the far wall are those two brothers, one in a wheelchair and the other not. The one in the wheelchair is popping wheelies, making kids laugh.

Rosa, that nice reporter who interviewed Emily, is serving cotton candy to anyone who wants some. Rosa looks up, smiles and waves to her. While Emily is scared about what might happen to her tomorrow and the next day, she wonders for a moment if this is what heaven will be like, surrounded by friends, laughing and everyone having a great time.

When they hear a quick purring humming sound, eveyone looks up into the sky, at the metal belly of the helicopter and the cameraman filming from above.

In unison, they all raise their arms in the air and wave, and after a minute the helicopter is gone, whooshing away, and the sky above is still and blue and cloudless. It is a sky that speaks of hope, of happiness. It is a sky that speaks of childhood, of lines on a sidewalk, of hopping, trying not to fall, and making it all the way to the end of something, which is really the start of something else.

While Emily, Garrett, Beth, and Holly start a new game of hopscotch, Emily looks over and sees her parents holding hands, talking to Garrett's mom and dad, and it looks like her mother might actually be smiling. Emily turns back to the hopscotch board. She is the first of her group of friends to hop. Her yellow mask covers most of her face. Her hair is almost gone now, just a yellow bandana around her head, and yet she feels as beautiful and graceful as an angel.

She tosses her stone marker. It lands on the three and she begins to hop. She laughs. She hops to the next box and the next and if she were not in a hospital gown, if she didn't have an IV in her right arm, and if she had a full head of hair again you would think she was like any other girl in the world. And for a few minutes today, at least, she is. She is. She is.

Steve Cushman earned an MFA from UNC-Greensboro. After working as an X-ray Technologist for twenty years, he currently works in the IT Department at Moses Cone Memorial Hospital. His debut novel, *Portisville,* won the 2004 Novello Literary Award. He's published a second novel, *Heart With Joy,* as well as the poetry chapbooks, *Hospital Work* and *Midnight Stroll.* Cushman lives in Greensboro, North Carolina with his family.